THE
ROOT OF HIS
EVIL

James M. Cain, born in 1892, was a recipient of the Mystery Writers of America Grand Master Award. Cain worked as a newspaperman in Baltimore and New York from 1917 to 1931. His first novel, *The Postman Always Rings Twice*, published in 1934, established him as the king of hard-boiled fiction. His work influenced writers of succeeding generations both in and out of the field of crime fiction. Albert Camus acknowledged his debt to Cain during the composition of his existentialist classic, *L'Etranger*. James M. Cain's novels stand alongside those of Raymond Chandler, Dashiell Hammett and Cornell Woolrich on the highest level of crime fiction. Cain died in 1977.

THE ROOT OF HIS EVIL

JAMES M. CAIN

Black Lizard Books
Berkeley • 1989

ISBN 0-88739-087-0
Library of Congress Catalog Card No. 87-72703

Manufactured in the United States of America

Part One:
THE GIRL
IN THE
BEANERY

Chapter One

It is hard to write on the deck of a sloop that is anchored here, off the Bay Islands, for if a swell from the Caribbean doesn't tilt the boat so the typewriter slides off the hatch, then a Bay Islander is aboard, telling about his ancestors, how they are really English and what they are going to do if Honduras tries to collect taxes. So the interruptions are many, but I want to tell my story, partly because to me it is my story, and partly to correct false impressions. Yes, I am Carrie Selden, the Modern Cinderella, but if a girl emerges who is different from the girl the newspapers pictured, then all I can say is that the newspapers printed a great many surprising things, and if they are shown up it is no more than they deserve. My story really begins, of course, with the appearance of Grant, but perhaps I should give some of my background, for it is not true that I was raised in an orphan asylum, and was scrubbing pots in the Karb kitchen at the time I met him.

I was born in Nyack, New York, and I don't know who my parents are, that much of the story is true. Also I was taken in by the orphan asylum, but the length of time I spent there was only six months. I then was taken in by Pa and Ma Selden, before I can remember, and they are the only parents I have ever known. The reason I don't know who my parents are is that the asylum had a rule that no information about parents would be given out, as it was better that the child have an entirely fresh start when it was adopted, rather than be the child of two families, and not really know where it belonged. But by the time I was old enough to be told that I was not the child of Pa and Ma Selden, and wanted to know who I really was, the asylum was not there any more, having been torn down to make way for a box factory, and I never was able to find but two of the matrons, who did not remember me very clearly, and did not know what had become of the records. Not knowing who your parents are is a matter worth a book in itself, but I shall not to say much about it, as I do not want to seem self-pitying. However, from my experience and certain traits of my character, I would say I must be Scotch. I am small, with yellow hair that has a touch of red in it, very large blue eyes, and a skin that has a tendency to freckle in the sun, as alas it is doing here on the sloop. My figure is very neat and pretty, and I am a little vain about it. But I am quite strong and nimble, and can do handstands and back flips, and often thought if I had to I could earn my living as an acrobat in a circus. I may as well confess that I am very careful in money matters, and always have been. From time to time certain of my friends have viewed this as a fault, and perhaps it is. But to me, money is something to be saved and used, not wasted.

I went to work when I was fifteen, that is, nearly ten years ago, because Pa Selden lost his farm to his sister, when she stood for interest on the mortgage, and while it was acceptable that Pa and Ma come to live with her, she wouldn't have me, as she had never approved of the adoption. So I had to find employment in Nyack, which presented some difficulties, as I had lived on the farm ever since I could remember, was only in the second year high school, and wasn't used to town ways. But as I have pointed out, I have always rejoiced in a strong body, and so was able to take a place as waitress in one of the hotels, although I had to misrepresent my age as eighteen. The salary was six dollars a week, but the first money I got was a dime tip. This I still have. At first I carried it tucked into a corner of my pocketbook, but now it is made into a little pendant, and hangs on a silver chain around my neck. While at the hotel, I enrolled for night classes at the high school, continuing the regular course, and graduated when I was nineteen. This was a year late, but it was not true that I write my name with a mark, as one newspaper said. I have a high school diploma.

Also, when I received my first salary at the hotel, I began a practice which I have never relaxed, which was to make a regular deposit in a savings bank. At first, I was able to spare only $1 a week, as I had to contribute to Pa and Ma Selden, since Aunt Lorna would not allow them any money for their needs. But after they died, when I had my nights free and could take extra work at the Diamond Cafe, I was able to increase my savings. And then when I came to New York and saw the night deposit boxes maintained by the banks there, I came to the resolution that has been an important part of my life: Let no working day go by which does not represent an amount saved. In New York I made my deposits nightly.

Thus it was that when I became twenty-one, I had a thoughtful day with myself, and decided that bigger things lay ahead of me than could be found in Nyack. This may sound conceited, but I had a little to go on. I had $855 saved up in the bank, representing principal and interest for six years, I had a knowledge of at least one business, and I had an education. So I began to consider New York, and after a trip down there to look around, I moved there, and two weeks later I took employment with the Karb restaurant chain, operating seventeen places in greater New York, in which I had a three-fold object. First, I wanted to enter a service big enough to hold a future by way of promotion, if I cared to remain there. Next, I wanted to save more money, in case I wanted to start a place of my own. Next, I wanted opportunity to study New York eating tastes, as well as restaurant methods, before coming to any decision at all. I had to start in one of the Brooklyn restaurants, and wait my turn for a Manhattan assignment, but I didn't have to wait long, as I agreed to transfer to the place on Lower Broadway, not regarded as very desirable. As the clientele was mostly from the Wall Street financial district, and as Wall Street is practically deserted after six o'clock, the restaurant did a luncheon business exclusively, so that the girls were only on call for four hours, hardly enough to make much. However, I made an arrangement with a cocktail bar within walking distance, near the City Hall, to work from three-thirty to six-thirty, and that way it came out very nicely. I worked from eleven to three at Karb's, and just had time to reach the Solon and change without an idle period. The pay at both places was sixty cents an hour, which came to about twenty-five dollars a week,

3

counting occasional overtime. The tips at Karb's came to about five dollars a day, about the same at the Solon, where although the rush time was shorter the patrons were a little more generous. I got my meals, breakfast and lunch at Karb's, and dinner at the Solon. So, exclusive of subway fare, which has to be subtracted, I made about eighty-five dollars a week in addition to my meals.

I debated where to live, and tried a furnished room for a few days, but there was something lonely about it, and besides I think any girl owes it to herself to live in a decent way. So I made inquiries, and finally located a hotel, the Hutton, on West 58th Street, which catered to women, and had a desirable suite which would shortly become vacant, consisting of living room, bedroom, bath and pantry, for $150 a month. I took it. Then I invited one of the girls at the restaurant, Lula Schultz, to share it with me. Yes, that is how I came to be associated with Lula Schultz, but let me say right now she was not as bad as the newspapers painted, even if she was a source of much trouble to me.

About the same time I thought it advisable to pay more attention to my dressing, and accordingly began to study the stock of the good shops, and presently bought myself two fine dresses, one for $59.50, and one for much more, more than I care to admit at the moment, but they were so becoming to me, and wore so beautifully, that I think they were worth what they cost. One was dark blue, the other dark green, and harmonious with my coloring. Miss Eubanks, the saleslady who sold me the green, made some hint about shoes, and when I drew her out, she told me that the foundation of all good dressing was fine shoes, which I never forgot. From that time on I paid money for what I put on my feet, but then again I have pretty feet.

■   ■   ■

Such was my general condition when I met Grant. I was twenty-two years old, strong, healthy and good-looking. I was saving $35.00 a week, I had ambitions for my future. Our manner of meeting was not in the least romantic, in fact the other way around. I remember the day: it was the 13th of August, two years ago, for it was the date of the

4

big organization meeting for the Karb waitresses, as it was the only one of the big chains still unorganized, under a big op deal that had been made by one of the four Karb brothers, one of whom had once been president of some printers' union. Indeed the local we were going to form, and all the big plans for the night, were very much in the air, and the girls could hardly talk about anything else. Personally, I was not greatly excited, but I felt if a union would do us any good we might as well have one, but possibly because I took such an unbiased attitude, the other girls kept gathering around me to know what I thought. Then in the middle of the lunch rush, one of them came back with a tray, and muttered out of the side of her mouth at us as she went up to the counter, "Company spy, girls, watch your step."

"Where?"

"By the rail, and he's asking me plenty."

"In the brown suit?"

I looked, but what I saw certainly didn't look like a company spy. He was big, and black-haired, and shaggy, and sunburned almost the color of copper. But the rest of them knew at once what he was, and began saying what they thought of him, and then Lula Schultz, my roommate, started for him. "Who do they think they are, snooping around on us? Can't we have a union if we want to? Isn't it in the Constitution or something?"

Lula is very impulsive, that is one of her main troubles, but another girl grabbed her. "Where you going?"

"I'm going to tell the bum where he gets off."

"And tip him to what we're doing?"

"What do we care?"

"You stop that, they'll know everything."

"We going to let them get away with this?'

Then one of them shoved her against the counter. "You stay right where you are. Let Carrie talk to him."

"That's it. Carrie can handle him."

"Sure, leave it to Carrie."

I didn't see that it made much difference what he was up to, but they seemed to place some kind of reliance in me, so it was up to me. One of the girls took the ammonia and cleared two or three places in my station. I mean she

5

wiped the tables with ammonia so the customers that were sitting there had to get up and leave, and another on duty as hostess that day, brought Grant over and sat him down, and I went and put the menu in front of him, and there we were. But if he had been inquisitive about the union, he didn't bring it up then. He seemed to be in a sulky mood, and after he studied the menu he looked up.

"What in the hell is Korn on the Karb?"

"Sweet corn on the ear, sir. Would you care for some?"

"No, just asking."

"The corn all comes from our selected farms, and the contract specifies that it must be pulled the morning of delivery, and arrive by special truck. If you like the dish, you might try the Mess o' Karb Korn on the a la carte—three large ears, cooked to order and served right out of the pot. The order includes drawn butter and a Karbtassle brush. It's really quite good."

"It's a socko sales talk."

"Would you care to try it?"

"I'll try it, but no silver handles, no drawn butter, and no Karbtassle brush. Now listen to what I tell you. That corn goes in the pot *in the husk*. Six minutes in the pot, put it on a plate, and bring it over. Give me a double hunk of regular butter, and *that's all*. The idea is, I don't want you to take no trouble with it. I want it as is. Do you understand me? No Karbnificence."

"Did you say—*in the husk?*"

"Indian."

"Oh."

"And besides it stays tender. And it stays hot. If Montezuma had 50,000 slaves to serve his table, you could certainly trust him on this."

"Yes, sir."

When I went over to the counterman they gathered around me like flies. "What does he want?"

"Korn on the Karb."

"Boil three, Charlie."

"Not so fast."

I then explained how the order was to be cooked, and Charlie's eyes almost popped out. He picked up three ears in the husk and shook his head. "One for the mule, girls. This is a new one we got."

That was a big laugh, but I kept thinking it was a very peculiar way for a company spy to act. So I decided to find out what he was, but first I would have to know his name. I filled a water glass and went up behind him. As I reached over him to set it down, I spilled a spoonful of it on his shirt, where his coat was hanging open. He jumped, but I had my napkin ready, and before he could say anything I was apologizing and wiping the water off. Then I pretended there was something on the inside of his coat, and began wiping that off. As I did so, I turned down the inside pocket, and there, sure enough, was his name, written in by his tailor. It said: Grant Harris.

I went to the pay telephone, took the receiver off the hook, and came back. "Pardon me, are you Mr. Grant Harris?"

He looked up, very surprised, and I stood right over him, looking down into his eyes so I could see everything they did. "Why yes. Harris is my name. Why?"

"They've been trying to locate you. Mr. Roberts is on the line. He wants to speak to you."

Nobody was on the line, but if he went over there and got no answer, I could pretend they must have hung up. What I wanted was to see how he reacted to that name Roberts when I spoke it that way, suddenly, because Mr. Roberts was general manager for Karb's, Inc. He didn't react at all. His face screwed up, and he looked at me as though I must be crazy. "Roberts? I don't know any Roberts."

"He's on the line."

"I don't know him, I didn't tell anybody I was coming here, so it must be some mistake."

"Do you want to talk?"

"What for?"

Not once did his eyes give that little flicker that a man's eyes will usually show when he is trying to hide something, so I felt all the more strongly that the girls were wrong about him. I went to the phone, pretended to hold a little conversation in case he was looking, hung up, and then went and got the corn. I put down the plate, butter, and the little platter with the three ears, still in the green husks. "May I remove the husks for you, sir?"

"No, thanks, but you can watch, so you'll know how next time."

"Yes, sir."

He began stripping the corn, very neatly, as though he had done it that way often. "...Why aren't you watching?"

It came like a shot, and his eyes were drilling me through. They were big and perfectly black, but now they were hard, as I found out they could be when there was reason. "I *am* watching."

"Me, you're watching, not the corn. I've been keeping book on you in that mirror."

"I'm sorry if I—"

"What is this, anyway? What was that phony call?"

Now there is such a thing as knowing when to stop the fooling, and besides I couldn't help having some admiration for the way he had caught me, even if I felt very silly. "All right, I'll tell you."

"Please do."

"They thought you were a company spy."

"Who did?"

"The girls. You asked some questions."

"Oh. So I did. Oh, now I begin to get it. That's why they're all watching us out of the corner of their eyes, is that it?"

"Yes. So they picked me to find out."

"Why you?"

"I don't know. They often rely on me."

"Because you're a pretty slick little spy yourself, maybe. How did you find out my name?"

"I found out all I wanted to know."

"Such as?"

"Anyway, that you're no company spy."

"You sure?"

"Yes, I'm sure. I don't think you're anything, much."

I only meant to get back at him for saying I was slick, but my remark had the most unfortunate effect on him. His eyes dropped, his face got red as mahogany, and he picked up the corn and started to eat it. I waited for him to say something, but all he did was gnaw around the corn, with even his neck getting red. I went and got his salad. When I got back, he was almost through his second ear. I picked up the other ear and stripped it exactly the way he had. "Just to show you I really was paying attention."

"Thanks."

"I never had it that way, but it looks good."

"What's your name?"

"Carrie. Carrie Selden."

"Well, Carrie, I think you're trying to be friendly, but you hit me below the belt. What made you say that? Was it just a crack, or—did you have something to go on?"

"I had to have *some* kind of comeback."

"Yes, but I'm thinking of something."

"What's that?"

"Those girls. Why did they pick you out?"

"Oh, they often do."

"Not for nothing. They thought you'd take my measure."

"They just thought I'd be careful."

He looked at me a long time, in a way that made me feel very peculiar, because to me at least there was something unusual about his eyes, something very warm and tender. Then he said: "Well, all I can say, Carrie, is that I find you very baffling."

"In what way, may I ask?"

"Everything about you seems delicate, and flowerlike, except that really you're very cold and knowing."

"I don't think I'm cold."

"Let's get on to this other thing. They're organizing here?"

"...Why?"

"There you go again, with that fishy look. You ought to do something about your eyes, Carrie. They give you away...Why? I'm curious, that's all. I'm no company spy, or anything like that. Just an interested bystander. But *interested*. I've got my reasons. I'm not just talking."

"What reasons?"

His face got very hard and bitter, and what he said next was almost between his set teeth. "Malice. Pure, unadulterated malice. They've got it coming to them, plenty."

"Who is they?"

9

"All of them. The system."

"I don't see any system."

"All right, I do. The foxholes improve your eyesight, maybe. Anyway, I've got interested in this social reform thing, and I'm going into it. I want to see how it works right from the beginning and here in this restaurant is a good place to start. I want to see how they go about it, this organizing, I mean. Does that clear it up?"

"You sound awfully sore about something."

"I am sore."

"Well—sure we're organizing."

"A.F. of L. or this other one?"

"...It's not the other one."

"How far has it gone?"

"It's all lined up."

"When does it pop?"

"That all depends. The meeting's tonight."

"Where?"

"Reliance Hall."

"Third Avenue, up near Eightieth?"

"Yes, it's over in Yorkville somewhere."

"Can I get in?"

"If you were a newspaper reporter—?"

"Ah, that's an idea."

"They're letting reporters in later, after the main part is over. I could get you in. Are you a reporter?"

"No, but I could muss up my collar. *Would* you?"

He made that sound very personal, so I quickly said, "Why not?" as though I didn't notice it.

"...Why did you make that crack?"

"If it bothers you all that much, I'll take it back."

"You can't. The truth is, I'm not anything, much."

"Well, my goodness, you're young yet."

"I'm twenty-seven. My farthest worth in the way of accomplishment was to get made a second louie in infantry...Napoleon conquered Italy at twenty-six."

"Maybe that wasn't so hot. Maybe Italy didn't think so."

"That's very sweet of you."

The girls lost interest when I said he was a reporter, as that seemed the simplest way out, but I could feel him following me about with his eyes wherever I went. More

10

customers came in, so we didn't get any more chance to talk. When he left, a half dollar was on the table.

Chapter Two

I tell all this to refute insinuations that were made, that I knew all about Grant, and took advantage of him from the start. The truth is I knew almost nothing about him, and what was said at our first meeting, it seems to me, proves that he acted very mysteriously with me, from the very beginning, and in spite of many peculiar hints, told me almost nothing about himself, and in fact concealed the main things from me. He did that, I know now, from modesty, and from being sick and tired of having people get excited over who he was, and from not being able to see that it made much difference anyway, since regardless of who he was he was not what he wanted to be, or even headed in that direction. However, I should like to make it clear that regardless of his motives, he did practice concealment. Now then, why didn't I compel him to be more candid? Why was I content to be kept in the dark? That part I shall explain too, when I get to it, and merely say at this point that there was a reason, equally strong to me as his reasons were to him, and yet nothing I need be ashamed of. I want it understood that until the terrible storm broke, Grant and I were practically strangers to each other, intimate and yet barely acquainted. It set me thinking about social customs in a way I never did before, of the importance of introductions and mutual friends and the various guarantees that people receive concerning each other.

■　　　■　　　■

We had the big meeting that night, and Lula and I went, and I must confess I wondered if Grant would come, which surprised me, for one does not as a rule think much about customers after working hours. Once in the hall, however, I was in the midst of events which transpired so rapidly

11

and unexpectedly that he was momentarily driven from my mind.

In general, I criticize all labor activities for being most inefficient and slipshod, and the meeting in Reliance Hall that night was no exception. There were 473 girls present, as my records later showed, all anxious to organize and get it over with. But just as most of them had found seats, word came that the girls of the Borough Hall restaurant in Brooklyn, who had previously been lukewarm, had decided to join, and were on their way over in a big bus, and that the meeting would wait for them. Why that had to be was never explained. So we marked time, and there were speeches, the gentlemen from the main council went into a huddle at one end of the platform, and nobody seemed really to be in charge, although a union lady from out of town was in the chair. All this gave time for factions to develop. Particularly there was a girl from the Union Square restaurant, by the name of Clara Gruber, who had a great deal to say about the full social value of our labor, which meant nothing to me, and in a few minutes, a lot of them were yelling for her to be president. This annoyed the girls from the lower Broadway place, who were going to put me up for president.

So very soon the meeting was split into two groups, one yelling for me, the other for Clara Gruber, and in a very disorderly manner, with names being called. So as soon as I could get the attention of the lady in the chair, I got up and declined the nomination, if indeed there had been any nomination, for there didn't seem to be any rules or motions or anything you could go by. This made things still worse, and the faction in favor of me threatened to secede. So then I hurriedly whispered to Lula and had her get up and say that if Clara Gruber was going to be president, then I had to be secretary-treasurer. My object in this was that I thought if our side had the money, it didn't make much difference who was president. So that satisfied Clara Gruber, and she was elected, and so was I, and we both went up on the platform, and the union lady stepped down, and Clara Gruber began making another speech about the full social value of our labor.

She was interrupted by the arrival of the girls from

Brooklyn. And then before she could get going, a little man in glasses came in, rushed up the aisle, and joined the huddle of the gentlemen from the main council of the culinary workers' union. And then he turned around, and without paying any attention to Clara Gruber, he clapped his hands for order, and announced very excitedly that Evan Holden, the big C.I.O. organizer, was going to speak to them, because on a question of that kind jurisdictional lines should be wiped out, and labor should present a united front. So then in came Mr. Holden, and behind him came about ten newspaper reporters, in the midst of whom was Grant. The reporters took seats down front, but I wasn't paying any attention to Grant at the moment. I was looking at Evan Holden. He was the special representative from International headquarters, and I must say I have rarely seen a more striking-looking man. He was over six feet tall, almost as tall as Grant, about thirty-five years old, with light hair and fair skin. His eyes were dark grey and very commanding. He had on a light double-breasted suit, which somehow brought out his heavy shoulders and the strong way he was built. But he walked rapidly like a cat.

He came marching up the aisle to the platform steps, and took these at one hop. Then he turned and faced the crowd and the girls began to cheer, so there was nothing for Clara Gruber to do but sit down. Then he began to talk. He didn't talk loud, and he didn't say anything about the full social value of our labor. He started off with jokes, and he had a sort of brogue which I took to be Irish, so in a minute he had them all laughing and orderly, and ready to listen. Then in the simplest way he told us what we were doing, about how Capital and Labor are really in a partnership, but it had to be an equal partnership, so it seemed that all we were really doing was demanding our rights. So pretty soon he had them very excited and then he said he wanted them to pass a resolution which was something about how we would all stick. And in order to get the resolution passed, he turned the meeting back to Clara Gruber, but from the quick way he peered at his watch I knew he had done his good deed and wanted to be on his way.

But instead of putting the resolution, Clara Gruber went on making her speech right where she was interrupted, and

13

I saw Mr. Holden begin to look annoyed because my faction began to make unfriendly remarks, and take another peep at his watch. But how well they would stick was something that had been worrying me, so I determined to get in it. I said, "One moment, Madame President," and before she could stop me I began making a speech of my own. I had never made a speech, but I thought if the way to get them interested is to tell them a joke, then I will tell them a joke. So I said:

"Once upon a time there were some mice that were going to bell a cat, but when the time came to do it they did not have any bell, but if they had had a little money maybe they could have gone out and bought one."

Instead of making them laugh this provoked a perfect storm, and there were screams from all over the house that it was distinctly understood no money was to be collected. I took the gavel, where it lay on the table, pounded with it and went on: "It has been proposed that you pass a resolution telling how you are going to stick, and I don't know what that's going to prove, but to me it will not prove anything except that you passed a resolution. But if you put up some money, then I'll believe you mean to stick, and so will Karb's and so will everybody."

Clara Gruber tried to get in it again, but they yelled her down. Even her own side was getting pretty sick of her by then. And then there came cries of "Let Carrie talk. Carrie knows what she's doing. Go on, Carrie, you tell us and damn right we'll stick."

So I went on: "Before I leave here tonight I'm going to collect one dollar off every one of you. The money will be deposited tonight in the Fiftieth and Seventh Avenue Branch of the Central Trust Company, receipt of deposit will be mailed to your president, Clara Gruber, but I'm going to collect it and anybody who refuses to pay is not going to be enrolled and had better not come around to me bragging about how they are going to stick."

There was a cheer for that, but I talked right through it. "Get out your pencils."

I waited till they got out their pencils. "Now take the leaflets that were distributed and write on the back as I direct. 'August 13th, received of —put your name in here—

14

one dollar on account of union enrollment dues.' Write that down, present it to me with the cash and I will sign it and it will be your receipt. Then form in line around the hall, pass by my desk, pay your dues, get your receipt, and be enrolled. While you are writing and forming in line I will ask Lula Schultz to step down to the drug store on the corner and buy me a small account book in order that the record can be kept straight."

Lula went out, and while they were writing and forming in line I noticed Evan Holden looking at me in a very sharp way. Then he came over, sat on the edge of the table in front of me, and leaned down close. "You're a pretty smart girl."

"Money is power. If they mean it, they can pay."

"We generally do it a little differently. The money comes from the outside, from the older locals. But your principle is correct."

"One dollar isn't much, but it proves they mean it."

Lula came back with the account book, and I got up and said they could begin passing by, and that then I thought it would be a good idea if they all went home, as there had already been enough talk. I didn't mean it for a joke, but they all laughed and clapped. He got up, still looking at me. "A smart girl and a pretty girl. Carrie, they call you. What's the rest of it?"

I told him and he said: "h'm."

■   ■   ■

I was kept pretty busy for the next twenty minutes, but by the time the last of the line was by most of the girls had gone home, except for Lula and four or five others from our restaurant, who were waiting for me. But Clara Gruber was still there, and Mr. Holden was still there too, but he wasn't looking at his watch any more, he was looking at me. And then at last Grant came edging up to me. "Hello."

"Hello."

"I got in."

"I see you did. Without any help from me."

"You certainly stirred things up."

"Just saying what I thought."

15

We talked a few minutes that way, not saying anything, and yet it was nice and friendly. Then he drew a long breath. "Do you suppose we could go somewhere for a cup of coffee or something, or maybe a little snack—there are quite a few things I'd like to ask you about it."

I was just opening my mouth to say I didn't see why not, but Mr. Holden must have been nearby, because he tapped me on the shoulder and then spoke to Grant. "Sorry, old man, but this little girl is going to be pretty busy tonight. We've only just started. Organizing a new union, you know—keeps us hopping."

"I see."

Grant looked disappointed, but I didn't believe one word of what Mr. Holden had said. What more did we have to do? I knew I was between two men who were interested in me, and I wanted Grant to put up some kind of a fight. But I would have died rather than let him know that, so I simply said: "I guess there's nothing *I* can do."

"I guess not."

Next, we were all edging toward the door, and Lula had me by the arm, all excited at what we had done, and Mr. Holden was with Clara Gruber, and I saw him hand her some money. I didn't know what for at the time, but later I found out that he said he thought it would be a good idea if she and the leaders went out and had a little supper together, but that it would look better if she did it rather than he, because she was president. So this appealed to her sense of importance, which was really quite strong, and she fell right into what was really a deliberate trap. Because as soon as we were out on the sidewalk he began waving for a taxi, and as soon as one came up he said: "Come on, girls, we're all going out for something to eat just to start the thing off right." Then he put Clara Gruber in the taxi, and Lula, and the other girls one by one until of course the taxi was all filled up. So then he told the driver to go on, to take them to Lindy's, that we would be right over in another cab. So then they drove off, and he and I got in another cab.

I knew perfectly well he and I weren't going to Lindy's, and under other circumstances I might have made objection, but there was Grant still standing on the curb and looking like a poor fish, and I was furious at him. So when Mr. Holden told the driver to go to the Hotel Wakefield I pretended not to notice, and when he waved at Grant and said, "Good night, old man," I waved and smiled too, just as though it was perfectly natural.

■ ■ ■

When the taxi moved off he asked me in the most casual way if I minded stopping by his hotel first, as he was expecting telegrams, and had to keep in touch. I said not a bit, and we rolled down Third Avenue talking about what a fine set of girls they were who had assembled in the hall. The hotel was on Sixth Avenue not far from where I lived, and when we went in there he went at once to the desk. They handed him some mail and telegrams and he tore one open. Then he came over to me, looking very depressed. "It was what I was afraid of. No Lindy's for us tonight, Carrie. I've got to stand by for a Washington call."

"It's all right."

"But we'll have our supper. Come on."

"If you're busy—"

"Don't be silly. We're having supper."

We went up in the elevator and entered his suite. He at once went in the bedroom and I could hear him phoning Lindy's with a message to Miss Clara Gruber that he had been unavoidably detained and would not be able to come. Then he came back and asked me what I would like to eat, and I said I didn't care, and he went back and ordered some sandwiches, coffee and milk. Then he called to know if I wanted something to drink, and I said thanks I didn't drink. He said he didn't either, and hung up. Then he came back. I was highly amused, and yet I felt some admiration for him. He had intended it that way from the beginning, and yet not one word had been said which indicated he had deliberately contrived to get me up here, and for some reason this made it much more exciting. I began to see that one reason men had previously left me somewhat indifferent was that they were extremely clumsy.

17

However, he continued to act very casual, and looked at his watch, and gave a little exclamation. "We can still get them."

"Get whom?"

"The Eisteddfod Strollers. They're broadcasting."

"At this hour?"

"It's midnight here, but it's nine o'clock in California. They're on tonight at KMPC, Hollywood."

He went to the radio and turned it on, and vocal music began to come in. "Yes, they're just beginning."

"Who are the—what strollers did you say?"

"Winners of our Welsh bardic contest called the Eisteddfod. They're terribly good."

"Are you Welsh?"

"A Welshman from Cardiff. A lot of us are Welsh in this movement."

"I thought you were Irish."

"The brogues are similar, but an Irishman isn't much good in a big labor union. He's too romantic."

"Aren't you romantic?"

I didn't know I was going to say that, and he laughed. "In some parts of my nature I might be, but not about labor. An Irishman messes things up, fighting for lost causes, exhibiting to the world his fine golden heart, but a Welshman fights when he can win, or thinks he can win. He knows when to fight, and he can fight hard, but he also knows when to arbitrate. It was characteristic of Lloyd George, another Welshman and a fine one. They called him an opportunist, but they won that war just the same. It's characteristic of John L. Lewis. A Welshman is a formidable adversary."

"Are you acquainted with Mr. Lewis?"

"Well, I hope so. I came up through the miners."

"To me he seems very theatrical."

"Like all specialists in power, he knows the value of underestimation of his abilities on the part of his adversaries. The newspapers call him the great ham, and I don't say he doesn't love the boom of his voice. But theatricality is not the dominant side of him. John L. is the greatest specialist in direct action that has ever been seen in the American labor movement, and to that extent I think he has a profounder understanding of labor than anybody we ever had, not even excluding Furuseth, who was a great man. What is a strike? They call it a phase of collective bargaining, but it is really coercion. It suits John L. to be thought a ham, for it distracts attention from his club. The club's the thing, just the same. He has a side though, that not many know about. At heart he's a boy and loves things like jumping contests. He can put his feet together and jump the most incredible number of steps on the front stoop of the hotel, or wherever it is. And over tables—anything. Or could. That was in the old days. I haven't seen him since the row with Murray."

"You went with Murray?"

"Aye, and there's a man, too."

"But aren't we culinary workers A.F. of L.?"

"Oh, there's plenty of fraternizing in areas where there's no real conflict, if that's what's worrying you. There is in any war."

"Are you in charge of our strike?"

"I wonder."

"Well—don't you know?"

"All I expected to do when the little fellow phoned me earlier in the evening, was go over and pull together a meeting he was getting somewhat worried about. But developments since then—"

"Meaning me?"

"Quite nice development, I would say."

He looked me over in a very bold way, and I could feel my face get hot, and I reached over and turned up the radio, as he had tuned it down during some announcement or other. The singing came through again, beautiful things I had never heard before, and I hated it when a waiter came in with our supper, and interrupted it. When the waiter had gone we began to eat the sandwiches, and Mr. Holden came over beside me. For the first time I felt a little frightened, and after a few minutes said: "I'll fix up the deposit slips."

I got out the money and counted it again, and put it in hotel envelopes, and then made out the slips, which I always carried with me. He watched and put the tray outside to be collected. The singers sang a song I loved, "All Through The Night." Mr. Holden came closer to me, and the music

19

seemed to be saying a great deal to him. We looked at each other and smiled. Then he put his arm around me. Then he took off my hat and laid it on the table in front of us. Then he kissed me. I was very frightened, and at the same time I was very limp and helpless. He kissed me again and I felt dreamy and carried away, and that time I kissed back.

■   ■   ■

I don't know how long I sat there in his arms, but it must have been quite some time, because my dress was all disarranged, and I didn't care whether it was or not, and I kept feeling that this was something I had been hungry for a long time. And yet at the same time there was something about it I didn't like. So long as the Strollers were singing, and I felt sad and at the same time happy, I was very glad about it all, but now there was nothing but swing music coming out of the radio it wasn't the same. I knew I had to get out of there, or something was going to happen that I was not in the least prepared for in my own mind, and that I did not want to happen. I loosened his arms and sat up, and began to shake my hair as though to straighten it out. "Do you have a comb?"

He got up and went in the bedroom. I grabbed my hat, the envelopes with the money in them, and my handbag, and scooted. I didn't wait for the elevator. As soon as I was in the hall I dived for the stairs, and ran down them, four or five flights. When I reached the lobby I ran out of the hotel, jumped in a taxi and told the driver, "Straight ahead, quick."

He started up, and I was so busy looking back to see if anyone was following, and straightening myself up, that I didn't notice how far we had gone. When we got to Fiftieth Street I told him to turn west, because I had to go to the bank before I went home. But it was a one-way street going east, and I paid him and got out to walk the one block to Seventh Avenue. I got to the corner, turned it, and started for the night deposit box. As I did so, somebody grabbed my arm from behind.

I jumped, shook loose and dived for the deposit box. I flipped the envelopes in, spun the cylinder, and turned around. If it was a bandit, I was going to scream. If it was Mr. Holden, I didn't know what I was going to do. It wasn't a bandit, and it wasn't Mr. Holden. It was Grant standing there and looking very sheepish. "I had an idea that money would be deposited."

"My, you frightened me."

"Feel like a walk?"

"It's terribly late."

"It's two o'clock—about the only time you *can* walk in this God-awful town. But that isn't the real reason."

"And what is the real reason?"

"You."

"Why didn't you say so?"

Chapter Three

We began to walk over toward the East River, but I wasn't any too friendly because while I was really glad he was there, I couldn't forget the way he had let me be dragged off from the hall without doing anything about it. So he began asking questions about the union, which I answered as well as I could. It was rather hard to explain it to him, however, as he apparently thought there had been a lot of preliminary phases, as he called them, all occurring in some extremely complicated way, although all that had happened was that some of the girls had become dissatisfied with conditions, and when they found out about the big op deal that had been made, had themselves gone to the union for help. Then the word was passed around, and one thing led to another, and it all happened very quickly with hardly any of the elaborate preliminaries that he seemed to think were involved. He kept asking me if I had read this or that book on the labor movement, but I hadn't, and didn't even know what he was talking about. So he died away pretty soon, and then he said: "I guess that about covers it. It's what I've been trying to find out."

"Then I'm very glad to be of help, if that's what you wanted because if it was really me you were interested in you took a strange way to show it."

"Well—here I am."

"Rather late, don't you think?"

"I told you. I like it this time of night."

"Between this time of night and that time of night three very fateful hours have elapsed. A lot can happen in that time."

"Happen? How?"

"There are other men in the world besides yourself."

"They don't start anything at Lindy's."

"I haven't been to Lindy's."

"You—?"

"Some people are more enterprising than you."

He stopped, jerked me by the arm and spun me around. "Where have you been?"

"Never mind."

"I asked you where you've been."

"With a gentleman at his hotel, if you have to know."

"So."

We went along, he about a half step in front of me, his head hunched down in his shoulders. Then he whirled around in front of me. "And what *did* happen?"

"None of your business."

We had reached Second Avenue by that time. He looked at me hard and I could see his mouth twitching. Then he turned around with his back to me and stood at the curb. I waited and still he stood there. "I thought we were taking a walk."

"We were. Now we're waiting for a cab."

"For what purpose, may I ask?"

"To send you home. Or to a gentleman at his hotel. Or wherever you want."

"Very well."

We stood there a long time, and still no cab came by, for it must have been getting on toward three o'clock. He lit a cigarette and something about the fierce way he blew the smoke out made me want to laugh. But I merely remarked: "If anything *had* happened I hardly think I'd be out here at this hour and under these circumstances—at least not *this* night."

"Why not?"

"I don't do things by halves."

I couldn't help saying it, he looked so silly. He sucked

at his cigarette and the light came up very bright. Down the street a cab appeared and when it got near us it cut in quickly and slowed down. He threw away his cigarette and waved the cab on. "We were taking a walk, did you say?"

■   ■   ■

We got over to Sutton Place and stood at the rail watching the sign come on and off, across the river. A fish flopped and we waited a long time hoping to see another. It was so still you could hear the water lapping out there. But no other fish appeared, and we started back. He hooked his little finger in mine and we swung hands, and it wasn't at all expert, but it was sweet and there was something about it that was exactly what hadn't been there on the sofa with Mr. Holden. A cop came around a corner, and we broke hands, but he said: "Don't mind me, chilluns," and we laughed and hooked fingers again. We came to a place where the sidewalk was barricaded over a water pipe or something, with two red lanterns on each end. Grant let go my hand, put both feet together and jumped over, then turned around to see what I was going to do. I pulled my handbags up over my wrist, took hold of my dress and held it away from me so it wouldn't fly up over my head, and then did a kind of one-hand cartwheel over the barricade. I came up right in front of Grant and made a little bow. He stared at me, then took me by the arms and pulled me toward him, and I thought he was going to kiss me but he didn't. He just kept looking down at me and his voice was shaky when he spoke. "Gee, you're swell."

"Am I? Why?"

"I don't know. Nobody else could have done that. Coming up cool as a cucumber that way with no foolish squealing or anything. And you've got no idea how pretty you looked—going over, I mean."

"That was nothing. I can turn back flips."

"I believe it."

We got to the Hutton and there was no doorman out there or anything, at that hour, and we stood there under the marquee for a minute. He took my arms again and seemed to be thinking about something. "Are you going to be down there today—for lunch, I mean?"

"Yes, of course."

"Can I come in?"

"It's a public restaurant."

"There's something that bothers me."

"What is it?"

"I want it back. I—don't want to feel that we started with me giving you a half dollar."

"Have we started?"

"I don't know what we've done. But I want it back."

Now that half dollar was much on my mind up there in the room with Mr. Holden. Because when I made out the slips for the union money I also made out the slip for my own regular deposit, and ordinarily that half dollar would have gone right in the pile with the rest of it. But for some reason I had kept it in the coin purse of my handbag. "How do you know I still have it?"

"Well, then—*if* you still have it."

"All right, then, I kept it. But I want it."

"Is that why you kept it?"

"It might be."

"All right, then, we'll make an agreement. *I'll* keep it. But I want it back."

"Very well, but I want *something*."

He looked a little funny, but fumbled around and then handed over his gold tie clip. "It—it seems to be about the only thing I have."

"I'm sorry, but I'm afraid that won't do."

I then held up my face in a very fresh way. He caught me in his arms and kissed me, and was very clumsy about it, but I kissed him back and held him there a long time. Then I drew back, and just before I skipped into the hotel I held out my hand and left the half dollar on his fingers.

■　　　■　　　■

I had to walk up, and when I went in our suite I didn't turn on the light and went carefully on tiptoe so as not to wake up Lula. But then I jumped because I could see her there, her eyes big and terrible-looking. I snapped on the light. She was sitting in her kimono facing the door and staring at me without saying a word. I spoke to her, and she began using

24

dreadful language at me in a kind of whisper. "But, Lula, what on *earth* is the matter?"

"You know what's the matter!"

"I don't even know what you're talking about."

"And you know what you been doing!"

"I haven't been doing anything."

"Oh, yes, you have." And she launched into the most terrible imaginary account of all that had taken place between me and Mr. Holden, and why I didn't go to Lindy's, and a great deal more that I prefer to forget. I thought it best to say that Mr. Holden had only wanted to take his calls, and talk a few plans with me while he was waiting, and that I had only stayed with him a little while anyway. "And, besides, I don't see what you have to do with it. I don't try to come between you and any of your friends, and certainly you have plenty of them." Which was the truth because Lula was not at all particular where men were concerned, and certainly went out with them a lot.

But nothing I could say had any effect on her, and she kept it up and kept it up, and it was easy to see that she was afflicted by some kind of jealousy which I didn't understand and still don't quite understand. But I think she had some kind of motherly feeling about me because she was several years older than I was, and it upset her to think I had at last taken some step with a man, as she assumed I had. She kept raving until long after daylight, and we got a call from the desk that we would have to keep quiet as people were ringing to complain. I didn't close my eyes until the sun was shining in the windows, and then when the nine-thirty call came I was almost dead from lack of sleep, but Lula wouldn't get up at all. "But Lula, you've got to go to work. And it'll look bad if somebody isn't there, the very day after we formed the union."

"To hell with the union."

"But we've all got to do our part."

"What I care about the union? Go on, let me sleep. Go on down and see your friend Holden. Stay out all night with him, stay out every night with him, do anything you please—but let me alone."

I went to work, and Lula didn't come, and I said she wasn't feeling well, and when I got back that night the hotel said she had gone and hadn't left any forwarding address. She didn't show up for work again. I would like this episode kept in mind, for it was the thing that caused most of my trouble later on, and if it had not been for Lula perhaps none of the rest of it would have happened. Or perhaps it would, I don't know. But Lula was certainly a large part of it.

■　　■　　■

Grant came for lunch that day, and the next, but was prevented from seeing me at night because of the tactics of Mr. Holden who didn't exactly take charge of us, or quite get out but kept having meetings at his hotel suite. He insisted that I attend every night, and Clara Gruber, and the girls from all the restaurants in the chain so that, as he said, we could discuss the minimum basic agreement we were going to demand from the company. Some wanted one thing and some wanted another, for example, seventy-five cents an hour wages, with "Please Pay Waitress" instead of "Please Pay Cashier," as it was felt the tips would be bigger if the waitresses presented the change, as they do in the hotels and higher class restaurants, and free uniforms. But I could see objections to all of these, from the management's point of view, and I didn't believe we could obtain them. What I wanted was the same hourly wages as we had, as what the restaurant paid us was only a small part of what we made anyhow, with a straight ten per cent charge for tips, as they have in a number of restaurants, with a minimum tip of twenty-five cents. Because in the first place it would be the customer who paid this, rather than the restaurant. And in the second place, it would come to more than the system we already had because what cut our tips down was the people who sat around for a long time occupying the chairs in our station during rush hour, and then leaving a dime tip. So I thought my plan would yield us quite a lot more, without costing the restaurant anything.

However, the others, and especially Clara Gruber, were all hot for *making* the management pay, and to my great surprise, Mr. Holden seemed willing to do whatever they wanted. This I could not understand until we were having some coffee in a restaurant one night, after the other girls had gone home. If he was going to see me alone, I had insisted that we go out. My running away that night, by the way, he had merely taken as a sort of joke and intimated that he would make progress with me yet. As to that, I had my own ideas, so I usually led the talk around to the union and our demands. His attitude he explained one night, first giving me a long wink. "Demands are poetry."

"They're what?"

"I'm surprised at the narrow limits of your soul. Let the girls demand. It expands their natures, makes them feel good, acts as a fine, stimulating tonic."

"But they won't get their demands."

"Oh—now you're speaking of settlement. That's reality."

"Isn't it *all* reality?"

"Not at all. They demand the stuff that dreams are made upon. They settle for what they can get."

"But that way we're sure to have a strike."

"No doubt we are."

"But that's terrible."

"Think, my pretty friend—it's August."

"Well?"

"It's hot. And a strike makes a holiday."

"They give vacations."

"Two weeks at Brighton, with mosquito bites. But a strike—there's something real. They have speeches and parades and lofty thoughts, and patriotic music."

"My but you sound cold-blooded."

"The main thing to remember in all labor matters, the point they all forget about, is the state of the weather. Cold-blooded? It's you that's cold-blooded, thinking always of the money. I remember that workers are human."

"They'll lose their wages."

"If they drew their wages, would they have their wages, will you tell me that? If they wind up broke in any case, why not have fun? Besides, it solidifies the union spirit."

"It's—wasteful."

"Your pretty dress is wasteful, for the matter of that."

"But it's *pretty*."

"So is a strike, in its way—a lot of girls, finding the courage to lift their heads at last. Perhaps they don't get all they want, but they had the fun of a fight. There's an element of beauty in it."

"To me it's just foolishness."

"Are you never foolish, Carrie?"

"Not willingly."

"A little folly would become you, I think."

■　　　■　　　■

The Saturday following our first meeting Grant came in for lunch again, and sat there very moody and didn't eat any of his Korn on the Karb, although the way he wanted it was rapidly becoming a restaurant joke. Then he wanted to see me that night, but I couldn't, and then he proposed that we spend the next day, which was Sunday, on the Sound. He said he had the use of a shack near Port Washington and a boat, and we could have a good time. Well, I thought, why not? I was all alone in the hotel now, and besides it was very hot. "Very well—if we get back by night."

"You have a date?"

"No, but there's a big meeting."

"Oh, the union."

"I'm an officer, you know."

"So you are. All right, I'll have you back in time."

So on my way up to the cocktail bar, I hurriedly bought a little sport dress and hat, a bathing suit, slippers and beach robe. Sure enough, next morning at nine o'clock the desk phoned that a Mr. Harris was in the lobby, and I went down wearing my sports outfit and carrying the beach things in a little bag that went with them. I supposed we were to take a train at Grand Central, but he had a car out there, a nice-looking green coupe. It was very pleasant riding along without any train to think about, even if the traffic was so heavy we could barely crawl. It was about eleven o'clock when we reached the shack, which was on a bluff above a little cove, with steps leading down. Well, he called it a shack, but I would have said estate, for it was a very fine place, with luxurious furniture on the veranda, and a big hall inside

28

with a grand piano in it and soft chairs all around. I couldn't help expressing surprise. "Did you say you just—borrowed this?"

"Belongs to some friends of mine."

"Do all your friends have such places?"

"I hope not. Some of them actually have taste."

"It's very luxurious."

"And very silly."

Now all of this was a complete evasion, as you will see, and I put it in to illustrate once more that during this period Grant was never frank with me. Also, he at once changed the subject. "What do you want to do? Swim, sail or eat?"

"Well—can't we do all three?"

"That's an idea."

He took me to what seemed to be a guest bedroom, showed me the bath and anything I might want, and went. I changed into my swimming suit, put on my slippers, and tied a ribbon around my hair. Then I put the bathing cap into the bag, slipped on my beach robe, and went out. I thought I looked very pretty, but I forgot about that when I saw him. He was ready and standing at a table flipping over the pages of a magazine. He had on a pair of faded blue shorts, big canvas shoes, and a little wrinkled duck cap with a white sweater over his arm. But he looked like some statue poured out of copper, and the few things he had on hardly seemed to matter. The deep sunburn was all over him, but that was only part of it. He was big and loose and lumbering, and yet he seemed to be made completely of muscle. The hunch-shouldered look that he had in his clothes came from big bunches of muscle back of his arms, and in fact his whole back spread out like a fan from his hips to his shoulders. His legs tapered down so as to be quite slim at the ankles and altogether he looked like one of the Indians he was always talking about. He turned, smiled and nodded. "Ready?"

"All ready."

"Come on while we still have a breeze."

He picked up a wicker basket and started for the veranda. I said: "Is that our lunch? Where did it come from?"

"We brought it with us."

"I thought I'd have to fix it."

"It's fixed."

I took hold of the handle too, we went out on the veranda, he picked up a paddle that was standing against a post, and we went down the steps of the bluff to the beach. The lunch he put in a little skiff that was pulled up on the sand, then he dragged the skiff to the edge of the water and motioned me into the bow. He gave it a running push and jumped in very neatly. Then he picked up the paddle and paddled out to a sailboat that was moored to a round white block of wood that he called a buoy. He made the skiff fast to a ring in the buoy, and we climbed into the sailboat. It had no bowsprit or anything, just a mast that went straight up from the bow, with one big triangular sail. He set down the basket, unwound some rope from a cleat, and began to pull up the sail. I helped him, and it took about a minute to get it up, and the boat swung slowly around and the sail began flapping in the wind. It was quite exciting. Then he went to the bow and cast loose, but held onto the short mooring cable that was attached to the buoy. Then he made me come and hold it, first showing me how to hold onto a cleat with the other hand so as not to be pulled overboard. Then he went back to the tiller. "All right, I'm going to put her over, and for just one second it'll slack. When it does, let go."

He put the tiller over, and the boat gave a lurch and all of a sudden I felt the cable slack. I let go, and when I looked up we were moving away from shore, toward the other side of the cove, with the sail out over the side, but still flapping. I climbed back to the middle of the boat. He kept watching and then he stood up. "Now I'm coming about. She'll go into the wind, the sail will flap like hell, then slam over, and for God's sake duck for that boom."

Suddenly he put the tiller over, the boat began to swing around and the sail set up a terrible flapping. Then without any warning it slammed across the boat, and I saw the boom coming and screamed and ducked. Then the sliding pulley to which it was attached by some ropes slid as far as it would go and caught it, and it filled, and the boat heeled over so far I thought we were going to upset. Then I saw we were pulling out of the cove very rapidly. Then the first swell from the Sound hit us and lifted us, and all sensation of being afraid left me, and I realized that for the first time in my life I was sailing, the way I had read about in books. I clapped my hands, and he laughed. "You like it?"

"I love it."

Chapter Four

We sailed quite a little while, and then he came about, and payed out some of the rope that held the sail, and we began to move again, but we didn't heel over. "Are we going back?"

"Just keeping in sight of home base."

"Make it tilt. I like that."

"We're running before the wind. We only heel over when we've got it across us. And it's a she."

"Oh, yes, of course."

It wasn't exciting the way it was before, but the water was smooth and green, so it was still quite pleasant. After quite awhile, he said: "Now, how about that lunch?"

"I'll get it ready."

"We'll both get it ready."

"But you'll have to steer."

"Steer what?"

"Why—her."

"You're the funniest sailor I ever saw. Haven't you noticed that for the last fifteen minutes we haven't had even the sign of the breeze?"

"Oh, *that's* why the water's so smooth."

"Yes, so now's our chance to eat. She'll drift, without much help from us."

■   ■   ■

So he kept one hand on the tiller, and we opened the lunch, sitting in the shadow of the sail. It was marvelous, with little thin sandwiches, stuffed eggs, and iced tea in thermos bottles. Every sandwich was in a little paper envelope marked: Loudet, Caterer. "Do you always deal with a caterer?"

"Him? Oh, he's just a Frenchman that puts up lunches."

"Rather expensive, I imagine."

"Is he?"

"So I judge. And I know about sandwiches."

"They're all right?"

"I'll say."

"Then eat 'em."

So we ate them, and then he lay there with his arm over the tiller and his eyes closed, smoking a cigarette. It was so hot little beads of sweat were dotted all over his upper lip, and not far from us were several other boats, their sails just hanging there as motionless as we were. But the water looked green and cool, and I longed to be in it. I got up, took the bathing cap out of my bag and put it on, then slipped off the beach robe and dived off. It felt so nice down there, and looked so pretty, with the sunlight filtering down, that I began to swim under water, and stayed down until my breath gave out and I had to come up. I looked back to wave at him, and to my surprise I was quite a distance from the boat, and he was standing there, his hand still on the tiller, swearing at me in a way I wouldn't have believed him capable of. He ordered me back at once, but I took my time, and finally he pulled me over the side. Then he explained that I had done a very dangerous thing in going so far, as a sailboat can't be maneuvered like a motorboat, and especially requires that one person always remain aboard it. So if anything had happened, and he had had to go overboard after me, a puff of wind might drift the boat away, and there both of us would be, out there in the Sound, two miles from land. I knew he was right, but didn't feel at all guilty, so I merely made a fresh remark: "And besides, the water is nice."

He sulked for a time, then unwound a rope and dropped the sail, then took another rope and tied it to a small wooden grating on the bottom of the boat and dropped the grating overboard, so it trailed in the water. "What's that?"

"That's our lifeline, so we don't get separated from our ship."

"How would be get separated from our ship?"

"Swimming."

"Are we going to swim?"

"Didn't you say the water was nice?"

He lifted his foot, put it square in the middle of my chest and pushed me over backwards. When I came up he was in the water beside me. We both laughed and splashed water at each other, but he made me hold onto the lifeline, and wouldn't let me swim off at all. I didn't mind. We both held onto the rope and floated side by side, looking up at the sky. Then he went under me and when he came up he floated facing me, so my head was at his feet, and our hands came together under water. I could feel his toes sticking out behind my head, but my toes stuck out near his ear, as he was a great deal taller than I. I moved my toe in front of his face and wobbled it, and he pretended he was going to bite it. So I pulled it away quick, but that pulled me off balance, and when I got straightened out again we floated for a little while, facing each other. Then he gave my hand a little tug, and my toes went past his head and his face began to come nearer and nearer. We hardly moved but our lips met and then he put his hand up to keep me from floating past him, and we lay there, his face against mine, just looking up at the sky. Then a swell lifted us and to me it was heavenly, but he whipped away from me as though he had been shot. He looked off to the west and then began going up the rope, hand over hand, and he was hardly in the boat before he motioned me and pulled me in after him. "Get all that stuff in the basket. Hurry up."

I still didn't know what was bothering him, but there seemed to be a great deal of activity in the boats that were near us. A man on the nearest one yelled at Grant. "What you going to do?"

"I'm going to run for it."

"You can't make it. I'm riding it out."

"Suit yourself. I'm going to run."

I was much mystified, and did as I was told, getting all our things in the basket, and yet I noticed that the water, while it was still green and the sun was out, was running long swells. By this time Grant was laboring to get up the sail. Pretty soon it was up and while there didn't seem to be any wind, it was flapping in a queer sort of way. He came back and put the tiller over, and suddenly we came about. The sail filled with a jerk, and once more we were running before the wind, except that this time we were lifting along with big swells that went past us, and yet carried us along. As we went past the nearest boat they were dropping the sail and running around highly excited. The man again called to Grant. "You can't make it, you'll crack up sure as hell on that shore."

"All right, so I crack up."

"Well, will you please tell me what it is?"

"Squall."

He was very grim, but except for the water I couldn't see any signs of a squall. Then, however, all of a sudden the sun wasn't shining any more and almost at once it turned cold as an icebox. Between the time Grant first ran up the sail and the time it turned cold was five or ten minutes, as well as I can remember. We had been about two miles offshore, and now we had covered about half that distance, headed for a point somewhat beyond the south of the cove. He put me at the tiller and went to the foot of the mast. "Hold her just as she is."

I held her and he kept looking back, and I heard him mutter: "Here it comes." I looked back and there on the water was a long streak almost completely black, and approaching us at a terrifying speed. When I looked again at Grant he was throwing a rope off a cleat, and the sail came piling down on the boom. He leaped back where I was and began hauling at the rope that held the boom. It came in with the sail dragging in the water, and just as it was in and Grant was wrestling the wet sail into the boat, it hit us. It was like a hurricane, with a splatter of big raindrops mixed with it, and the swells that were racing past us suddenly turned foamy white.

"Put her down!"

He pushed the tiller hard over, and we lurched straight for the cove, the wind and swells carrying us along without any sail at all. The mouth of the cove, I would say, was about a hundred yards away, and we covered the distance in almost no time, scudding rapidly past the grass which was flattened down on the water by the wind and looked white, not green, as indeed everything looked queer, for while it was almost dark a peculiar light seemed to be everywhere. As we entered the cove the first lightning flash came, followed almost at once by a clap of thunder. Not far away I could see our buoy, with the little skiff bouncing up and down on the waves. He took the tiller and pointed for the buoy, yet not quite for it. "Hold her that way till I tell you, then put her up, *hard*. Have you got it? I want to overshoot the buoy, then hit it upwind."

"I've got it."

He went to the bow and lay down with his head hanging over. I headed as he said, and we bore down on the buoy at terrifying speed. When we were almost on it, and yet a little to one side, he called, like a shot: "Put her up!"

I jammed the tiller over hard, and we came lurching around on the buoy, with the swells slamming us sidewise. Then we seemed to hesitate for a moment, but that was enough for him. He made fast, and we whipped around so the boat strained on the mooring cable with a jerk that almost threw me overboard. The wind tore at our faces and the little skiff began slamming and bumping alongside. "Come on!"

He grabbed the basket, we jumped into the skiff, and he cast off. He grabbed up the paddle, and spun us bow on to the shore. It was out of the question to paddle for the foot of the stairs for the wind was driving us about fifty yards farther down, and he didn't even come back to the stern. He stayed in the bow using the paddle to keep us headed right, and it was only a few seconds before he jumped overboard, grabbed the bow of the skiff and ran it up on the shore with me, the basket, and all right in it. "Out!"

As I jumped out the sheet of rain hit us. He grabbed the basket and we raced into the rain for the stairs, then up and over the grass to the veranda. Lightning and thunder crashed as we ran up the stairs. We stood there panting and looking out at it.

When he got his breath he turned to me and half laughed. "Were you scared?"

"No."

"I was."

He put the paddle away, then carried the basket inside and I went in too. Suddenly he dropped the basket and caught me in his arms. "So scared, Carrie—I didn't know what to do."

35

"On account of me?"

"Who else?"

Next thing we were sitting on the big sofa, and he was holding me very close and we were watching the rain come down in sheets. He took off my bathing cap and began running his fingers through my hair. I pulled off the ribbon and it fell all over his bare shoulder. We sat there a long time that way, and every time the thunder crashed I was a little nearer to him and I felt terribly happy and didn't want it ever to stop raining.

■   ■   ■

But it stopped, and the sun came out and when we went outside to look at the rainbow there were the Sunday papers, all wet and soggy on the grass where we hadn't seen them in the morning. We took them in, and the middle sections weren't so wet, and we looked at them for a while and then turned on the radio. I went to the powder room to straighten up—then decided to dress, and went to the bedroom where my things were. When I came out he wasn't the same any more. He began marching around, then said he had to stow the sail, and went out. I felt it had something to do with the radio. I turned it on and noticed the station, but Bergen was on and that didn't seem to explain anything. The sail took a long time. When he came in he went in and changed into his regular clothes, then came out and kept up that restless tramping around.

By now it was getting dark and I kept thinking of the meeting. "Isn't it time for us to be starting back?"

"Is it?"

"It must be getting on toward seven o'clock."

"H'm."

He sat down and began to glower at his feet. "I've been organizing a junior executives' union. Or trying to."

I didn't think it was at all what had been bothering him, but just to be agreeable, I said: "Are you a junior executive?"

"Me? I'm nothing."

"Oh, I see."

"Yes, I'm a junior executive, God help me. I've got a desk, a phone extension and a title. Statistician. You can't beat that, can you? It sounds as important as a member of the Interstate Commerce Commission. But all I can make out of it is slave. In the Army we had slaves and overseers, and I was both. Here I'm one, but I'm supposed to pretend I'm the other. But I've accepted my lowly lot. Did you hear me? I've accepted it."

"I don't accept my lowly lot. I'm nothing too. I'm only a waitress, but I have ambitions to be something more."

"The emancipated slave wants to drive slaves."

"All right, but they can get emancipated if they've got enough gump."

"But you still see no objection to slavery."

"It's not slavery."

"Oh, yes, it is, yes, it is."

"To me, it's work."

"Suppose you wanted to do work that didn't pay, and yet they made you be an office worker?"

"All real work pays."

"Oh, no. That's where you're wrong. Some work doesn't pay. And yet you want to do it, and you can choose between going to them with your hat in your hand—a junior executive. Either way you're their slave."

"Whose slave?"

"All of them. The system."

"I don't see any system. All I see is a lot of people trying to make a living."

"Well, I see it. And I accept it. But I'm going to make them accept it too—accept the other side, show them there's two sides to it. I've been trying to organize a junior executives' union."

"Any success?"

"...No!"

"Why not?"

"They won't admit they're slaves!"

"Maybe they're not, really."

"Maybe the dead are not dead, really. They want to pretend they're something they're not—white-collar workers thinking they're part of the system, on the other side. They think they're going to be masters, too—"

"Like me."

"Like you, and a fat chance—"

"You can just leave me out. I don't want to drive any slaves, but one day I'm going to *be* something, and I can't be stopped—"

"You can be, and you will be!"

"Oh, no. Not me."

There was a great deal more, all the same vein, and finally I got very annoyed. "I don't like this kind of talk and I wish you'd stop."

"Because at heart you're a cold little slave-driver."

"No, that's not it at all."

"And what *is* it?"

"Because you sound so weak."

He sulked a long time over that and then he said: "I *am* weak. You're weak—"

"I am *not!*"

"We're all weak, that's why we've got to organize, it's the only way to beat them!"

"All right, maybe I'm weak, I'm only a girl that came to the city a few months ago, and I'm nothing to brag about. *But I'd die rather than admit it!*"

"I admit it! I admit the truth! I—"

"You stop that kind of talk right now! The idea! A big, strong healthy galoot like you, only twenty-seven years old, admitting you're licked before you even start!"

I was very angry. It was completely dark by now, and I knew I could never get to the meeting, so didn't even say any more about it. I knew that he still wasn't talking about what was really on his mind, although he certainly felt very strongly about this labor business, but in some way I felt it was important and I wanted to have it out with him.

■   ■   ■

When I called him a big strong galoot, I yelled very loud, and then he seemed to realize that there might be neighbors, and subsided for a time. I went out in the kitchen to see what there might be to eat. The icebox was empty, but there was plenty of English biscuit and canned things, so I made some canapes and coffee and served them on a table in the living room, although I had to use condensed cream with the coffee. He gobbled it down, as I did, for we were very hungry. Then I took the dishes out, and he came and helped me wash them, and then we went back. I took his hand in mine. "What on earth is the matter with you anyway? Why don't you tell me what it's all about—what it's *really* all about?"

He gulped, and I saw he was about to cry, and I knew he wouldn't want me to see him doing it. I snapped the lights out quick, and went to the door of the veranda. "Let's sit out here. It's such a pretty night."

It *was* a pretty night, with no moon but the stars shining bright and frogs croaking down near the water. We sat in a big canvas porch seat and I took his hand in mine again. "Go on. Tell me."

"What the hell? You want the story of my life?"

Now right there was where I should have said yes, I want the story of your life, it's most important that I know the story of your life. But at his words something like a knife shot through me. Because if he told the story of *his* life I might have to tell the story of *my* life, and I didn't want to have to say I had been an orphan, and I didn't know who I was, that I didn't even know my proper name. Perhaps you think this is far-fetched, but there are many of us in that situation in the world. We form a little club, and if you ever meet any of them they will tell you the same thing: it is a terrible thing not to know who you are, a secret shame that gnaws at you constantly, and all the more because you are helpless to do anything about it. So I merely said: "Not if you don't want to."

"I'm—just no good, that's all."

"Some people might not think so."

"Oh, yes, if they knew it all."

"Most of the time I think you're—a lot of good. And fine inside, I mean. But I don't like it when you talk this way. I don't mind what you are. I don't mind if you're never anything—of what you mean. But I hate it when you stop fighting. That's the main thing—to do your best."

"I'm blocked off from my best."

Again, what was he talking about? I didn't know, and for my own reasons, I was afraid to ask. So I merely patted his hand and said: "Nobody can be blocked off from their best, if they really try. It's got to come out."

He put his head on my shoulder, and we sat a long time without talking, and then he went to the end of the veranda and sat for awhile with his back to me, looking out over the water. Then he came and stood looking down on me. "There's one way I can get back at them."

"How?"

"By marrying you."

It was like a dash of cold water in the face somehow. Up to then, in spite of all the talk he had been indulging in, I had felt very near him, but now I felt very queer, and must have hesitated for a time before I said anything. "Is that the only reason you want to marry me? To get back at them?"

"Well—let's say to get clear of them."

"To show your independence?"

"All right, put it that way."

"It doesn't interest me to be the Spirit of '76 to your little revolution—whatever it's about, as I haven't found out yet."

"What do you mean by that?"

"There's only one reason I'd marry you, or anybody. If you loved me, and I felt I loved you, that would be enough reason. But just to get back at them—well, that may be your idea of a reason, but it's not mine."

"There's plenty I haven't told you."

"I doubt if I'd be interested."

I went in, put my wet bathing things back into the bag, put on my hat and went out. He was sitting on the step. "Where are you going?"

"Well, there seems to be a town or something over there, so I thought I'd take the train back. I was supposed to be brought back long ago, but nothing seems to have been done about it."

He threw my bag into a corner, took off my hat and sat me down in the canvas porch seat. Then we started arguing again, and were right back where we started.

■   ■   ■

We argued and argued, and it was dreary and didn't make any sense, and he said of course he loved me, and I said he didn't say it the right way. Then he said his vacation started the next day, and we could have a two-weeks' honeymoon, and I said I didn't see what that had to do with it. Then the frogs stopped croaking as though somebody had given them a signal, and it was so still you almost held your breath and everything we had been talking about seemed unreal, and all that mattered was that he was there and I was there, and peace came down upon us. And after awhile I said: "How much do you make?"

"...Hundred bucks a week."

"All right, then, I make eighty-five. That's enough."

"Do you mean yes."

"I might as well. I really want to. Do you?"

"You know I do."

"Then yes."

Next thing I knew, the sun was shining and I was lying there under a blanket, and he was shaking me. "Breakfast's ready."

I got up and went inside. He was all shaved and fresh-looking, but my sports dress was wrinkled, and my eyes were red and my face shiny, and my hair all rough and ratty. I took a bath, gave the dress a quick press with an electric iron that was there, and made myself look as decent as I could. Then we had the toast and coffee he had made, and when we got in the car the dew was still on the grass. We were before the big Monday rush, and made good time. We parked near Brooklyn Bridge and went over to the City Hall and got married. We were the first couple. We got in the car again and started uptown. I looked at him and realized I had never yet called him Grant, and yet he was my husband.

Part Two: KNIFE UNDER THE TONGUE

Chapter Five

We drove up to the Hutton, and I went up and packed and then came down and checked out, and paid with a check. He put my things in the car, and we drove over to his apartment, which was on East 54th Street. It was in a regular apartment building and had a large living room with a view clear over to Queens, and dining room and kitchen, and seemed a great deal more expensive than anybody could afford who made only a hundred dollars a week. But that wasn't what struck me about it. It was the strangest place I had ever been in, and yet I knew it was interesting and in very fine taste. Except for the furniture itself, which was comfortable and of good quality, everything in it, even the rugs, was Indian. There were Mexican serape, all very beautiful, hanging on the walls, as well as pictures by Mexican artists, mainly, as I later found out, Rivera and Orozco, all of Indians. There were Navajo rugs scattered around, and Indian silver and gold work, and on the wall a framed collection of arrowheads, ranging in size from tiny little red ones, which had been used to shoot birds with, up to big spear heads, and all arranged beautifully, in order of size, in white cotton batting with a glass frame over them. Then off on a table, under glass, there was a collection of stone instruments, which I later found out were what the Aztec priests had used to hack out the hearts of the sacrificial victims. However, there was something very beautiful about them, made as they were out of a black stone called obsidian, which was capable of being sharpened, as Grant once showed me, merely by holding it in water so that the oxidation or something brought it to a fine edge.

All this, however, I only partly saw, except to realize I was in a most unusual place, and also to realize that there

45

was something back of all this wild talk of Grant's that I did not in the least understand. He had the boy take my things to the bedroom, and then began walking around much as he had the evening before. Suddenly it was dismal and hot, and sticky, and completely different from what a bride's first day is supposed to be. However, I merely said: "It must be getting on toward eleven, so I think I had better go to work."

He hardly seemed to hear me. "Ah—what was that?"

"I say it's time for me to go to work."

"Oh. I suppose so."

"Well—shall I come back here then?"

"Why—yes, of course."

"May I have a key?"

"Why—certainly. Here, take mine."

■　　■　　■

I usually went to work on the subway, but I felt so miserable I took a taxi, first taking care to note the number of the apartment house, which made me feel still worse, as it was really supposed to be my home, and yet I had to remember it as though it was the address of some stranger. I cried in the taxi all right, and I was still crying when we came in sight of the restaurant. Then I saw it was being picketed, with a lot of the girls out there carrying placards, and arguing with people that started to go in. So I knew the strike had come as a result of the big meeting. But I was too sick at heart even to think about the union, or anything, and I told the driver to go on without stopping, and then I told him to turn around and take me back where he had picked me up.

■　　■　　■

He had to go down to the Battery to turn around, and then was when I heard newsboys screaming the name Harris and saw the big headlines. I bought a paper out of the cab window and there it was:

HARRIS JILTS DEB, WEDS WAITRESS

Underneath was a big picture of Grant, with the caption Heir to Railroad Millions, and a smaller picture of a girl named Muriel Van Hoogland, with a brief item in very big type saying their engagement was announced last June, the wedding to take place in September, but that when she flew in from California that morning, she found he had just two hours before married me. I began to see things a little more clearly, or thought I did. I looked to see if there was any more, but there wasn't except for a small item about the Karb strike. It had started, apparently, only a few minutes before I drove up there. The demands adopted at the big meeting had been presented to the management, which refused even to consider them at all, whereupon the girls had been called out on strike.

By now, I realized that except for the coffee at the shack, I hadn't had anything to eat, so instead of going at once to the apartment, I had the driver let me out at Times Square, and went in a restaurant for a sandwich. But while that was coming I went to the phone booth and called NBC and checked on the programs that had gone on ahead of Bergen on that station. And one of them was the young man who does interviews with people boarding planes at Lockheed Airport, in Burbank, California.

■   ■   ■

When I came out on the streets again there were later editions, with longer items in them. One was an interview with Muriel Van Hoogland, in which she said she didn't care a bit, and then burst out crying and slammed the door in the reporters' faces. One was about me and my work at Karb's and in the headline of that occurred for the first time the nickname, Modern Cinderella, which stuck. So by now I was not only feeling miserable, but afraid and worried, and I wanted time to think. I didn't feel glad I had married a rich man. That part hardly entered my head, important though I hold money to be. I merely felt in some bitter way that I had been made a fool of, and when I ate my sandwich I walked up to the Newsreel Theatre and went in and sat down. There was nothing about me on the screen that day. I suppose it was too soon, though there was plenty later. I don't know how long I sat there, but finally it all seemed to focus that I had to have it out with Grant, and yet I even hated the idea of going back to the apartment. So after a long time I left the theatre, and it must have been three or four o'clock.

When I came out into the sunshine, I was startled to see my own picture in the papers, very big, with Grant's picture much smaller, and Muriel Van Hoogland's just a little circle down at one side. It was the picture I had taken when I graduated from high school in Nyack, and that meant it must have come from there, and that frightened me. And sure enough, there was a whole long item about the orphan asylum, and being a waitress in the hotel, and all the rest of it that I had wanted to keep to myself.

But what made something turn over inside of me was the big headline at the top of the page:

CINDY EMBEZZLED, CHARGE

And the main story was all about how Clara Gruber said I had absconded with the union funds, and had sworn a warrant out for my arrest.

■　　　■　　　■

I went to a drug store and called the Solon, and told them I was quitting. I didn't take a cab over to the apartment. I didn't want to go that fast. I went clumping over on my two feet, and the nearer I got the slower I went. I went up in the elevator, let myself in, and Grant was in the bedroom making a phone call. It took several minutes, and seemed to be about somebody that was ill, whom I took to be Muriel Van Hoogland, but that was a mistake. I sat down and waited. He hung up, and came out and began marching around again, and seemed to be under a great strain. He went to the window and looked out. "It's hot."

"Quite."

"By the way, I was thinking of something else this morning when you went out and didn't realize what you meant. You don't have to bother about that job. There's no need for you to work."

48

"I didn't."

"You—oh. That's good. It's terribly hot."

"They're on strike."

"Who?"

"The girls. The slaves. Remember?"

"Oh. Oh, yes."

The bell rang, and he answered it. It was a reporter who had come up without being announced. "Well—I suppose you'd better come in."

I remembered what Muriel Van Hoogland had done, and thought that was a pretty good idea myself. I went and slammed the door in the reporter's face, then went back and took my seat again. "Now—suppose you begin."

"About what?"

"About all of it."

"I don't quite know what you mean. If there's something on your mind suppose *you* begin."

"Who was that you were so concerned about just now?"

"My mother. This thing seems to have upset her."

"You mean your marriage?"

"Yes, of course."

"To a waitress?"

"—All right, to a waitress, but if I'm not complaining, I don't see that we have anything to discuss."

"I do, so we'll discuss. Who are you, anyway?"

"I told you my name. In case you've forgotten it, you'll find it on the marriage certificate. I believe you took it."

"You seem to be a little more than Grant Harris, Esquire. May I ask who the Harrises are—why the newspapers, for example, give so much space to the marriage of a Harris to—a waitress?"

"U. S. Grant Harris, my grandfather, was perhaps the worst scalawag in American history. He stole a couple of railroads, made a great deal of money—$72,000,000, I believe was the exact figure—and died an empire builder, beloved and respected by all who knew him slightly—or at any rate by the society editors. He left two children— my father, Harwood Harris, who died when I was five years old, and my uncle, George Harris, head of Harris, Hunt and Harris, where I have the honor to be employed. My uncle carries on my grandfather's mighty work—he stole a railroad in Central America only last week, come to think of it. I could have told him the locomotive won't run, now that all the wood along the right-of-way got burned off in a mountain fire a few months ago, but he didn't consult me, and—"

"Never mind the mountain fire. Whose house was that—where we spent the day yesterday?"

"...My sister's, Mrs. Hunt's."

"Why did you say it belonged to a friend?"

"Well—of course, it really belongs to her husband. I hope I can call Hunt a friend."

"I'd call him a brother-in-law."

"I guess he is, but I never think of him that way."

"Why didn't you tell me all this sooner?"

"Well, you never asked me, and—"

"And, in addition to that, there was this little matter of—Miss Muriel Van Hoogland. Who is she?"

"Just a girl."

"Whom you had promised to marry?"

"That was all my uncle's doing. My uncle continues another pleasing custom of my grandfather's by the way—the negotiation of what he calls favorable alliances, meaning marrying his nephews off to girls who have money. It wouldn't have meant anything except that my mother let the wool be pulled over her eyes and before I knew it, mainly to make her happy, I had got myself into something pretty serious."

"And then Muriel went west?"

"Yes, that was in July."

"To buy her trousseau?"

"That I don't know."

"Oh, I think we can take it for granted, that to be worthy of a Harris, Muriel would buy her wedding clothes at Adrian's."

"What she did in California I don't know and I'd rather we took nothing for granted, if you don't mind."

"And then?"

"And then *you* came along."

"And then true love was so irresistible that you left Muriel stood-up at the airport and married me, is that it?"

"I guess that about covers it."

"Well I don't. You didn't say anything about love when you asked me to marry you—not at first, and it hurt me, and I ought to have known that any other reason was an insult, and—"

"Is a marriage proposal an insult?"

"Oh, it can be, even from a Harris, if that one thing isn't there—"

"Don't you *know* how I feel about you?"

"Sometimes I know—or think I do. But that wasn't why you asked me. It was all about the system and getting back at them, whoever 'they' are. Is that the only reason you wanted me, so you could get back at your uncle for trying to make you marry Muriel?"

"No!"

"Then *what* was it?"

"It would take me a week to explain it to you."

"I've got a week."

"They won't let me do what I want to. They—"

"And who is 'they'?"

"My uncle!"

"And your mother."

"We'll leave my mother out of this."

"Oh no, we won't."

"I tell you my mother has nothing to do with it. If everybody in the world were as fine as she is—the hell with it! I—I've got to go see how she is. She's my mother, can't you understand that? And she's sick. I've—I've brought this on her. I—"

He started for the door but I was there first. "And I'm your wife, if you can understand that. And you've brought this on *me*. You're not going to your mother. I don't care how sick she is—*if* she's sick, which I seriously doubt. You're staying here, and we're going into it. I told you—I've got a week, I've got a lifetime. They won't let you do what you want to do, I think that's what you said. What is it you want to do?"

I still stood there by the door, and he began tramping up and down the room, his eyes set and his lips twitching. He kept that up a long time and then he dropped into a chair, let his head fall on his hands and ran his tongue

51

around the inside of his lips before he spoke to stop their twitching. "Study Indians."

"You—what did you say?"

He leaped at me like a tiger, took me by the arms and shook me until I could feel my teeth rattling. "Laugh—let me hear you laugh! I'll treat you like a wife! Just let me see a piece of a grin and I'll knock it down your throat so fast you won't have time to swallow it! Go on—why don't you laugh?"

"Is that why you have all these Indian things here?"

"Why do you think?"

"And you want to read books about them? I still don't quite understand it."

"What do I care whether you understand it or not, or anybody understands it? You don't study Indians out of books. You study them on the hoof. You go where they are, and—oh, God, what's the use?"

"You mean in—Oklahoma?"

"If you knew anything—or if you or *any* of them knew anything—you'd know that all the Indians aren't in Oklahoma. More than half the population of his hemisphere is Indian—millions and millions of them—they're the one surviving link with this country's past—they're anthropologically more important than all the tribes of Asia put together and—skip it. I'm sorry. It would be impossible to make you understand it, or any of them understand it, and I apologize for even trying."

"You study them—and then what?"

"Write a book. That's all—just a book."

I sat down and then looked around the room at all the things he had in there and after awhile I got up and walked around looking at them one by one. There were little typewritten labels on most of them which I hadn't noticed before, telling exactly where they came from, what their use was and what their names were in Indian languages and in English. Then I walked over to the big built-in bookcase that filled one side of the room and pulled out one or two books and looked through them. They were different from any books I had ever seen—most of them were bound in leather, some of them in parchment, and they were filled with all sorts of footnotes and scientific references. I knew then at least what he was talking about, the kind of books he wanted to write anyway, even if I had never read any books like that, or even knew there were such books. But there was still more I had to find out. "Why won't they let you—study Indians?"

"Costs money."

"In what way?"

"All you have to have is an expedition, a flock of assistants, an army of porters and a boatload of equipment. It runs into money, big money. And I've *got* money—all the money it takes—or will have some day, when George Harris is no longer trustee. That's why I said I'd marry that Muriel idiot. I thought if I did that George might kick in, but when he got coy about it I knew that was just a dream."

"You didn't make the money."

"Neither did George Harris. Neither did my grandfather. He stole it—and a lot I care. But isn't it better to have it put to some decent use? Am I supposed to jump up and cheer when George Harris uses it to win a race with one of his yachts? All right, you want to know why I hate the system—any system's wrong that lets useful wealth be wasted so George Harris can sail yachts—the Alamo, the Alamo II, the Alamo III, and the Alamo IV—aren't they a lovely end-product for a civilization? For them men sweat and walk tracks in blizzards and tap flanges and get killed in wrecks, and for them I have to give up something that's worth doing."

"And to break that system you tried to organize a junior executives' union?"

"Anyhow, I tried to do *something!* All right, George made me a junior executive. The day after I got out of Harvard he had a job waiting for me—a swell job where I can learn the business from the ground up, so one day I can acquire a knowledge of stealing, so I know how it's done. I beat that rap by going in the Army. But Okinawa didn't last forever and pretty soon here we were again, and this time I told him O.K. and so I don't disgrace him when I board his yacht he gives me an allowance of $200 a week. And so I get thoroughly integrated, as he calls it, he tells me to marry Muriel. Well, you're right. Going after George by organizing an office-workers' union is like hunting an

53

elephant with a cap pistol. But a kid with a cap pistol is fire-arm conscious, at least. I'll get him. I'll get him yet."

"I see. Marrying a waitress was merely exchanging a cap pistol for a pea shooter. They're not much good against elephants either."

"Listen, I've got you, and you're my first step in cutting loose from George, his yachts and everything he stands for."

I felt sick and queer and frightened. We sat there for a time in the half-dark, for it was now well after six, and then it was my turn to begin walking around. I kept passing the bookcase, and little by little it crept in on me that this man was my husband and that, in spite of my pride, I had to help him fight through somehow, even if I didn't quite understand what it was about or believe in it at all, for that matter. I went over, sat down in his lap and pulled his head against me. "Grant."

He put his arm around me and drew me close to him. "You never called me that before."

"Do you want me to?"

"Yes."

"I think the Indians are swell."

"I think you mean you like me."

"I more than like you, or will, if you'll let me. But that isn't what I meant, and that isn't what you want me to mean. I don't know much about Indians, or this book—"

"It'll be a hell of a book."

"That's it—tell me about it."

"It'll take me ten years to write it but it'll really be a history of this country that everybody else has missed. Listen, Carrie, they've all written that story from the deck of Columbus' ship. *I'm* going to write it from San Salvador Island, beginning with the Indian that peeped out through the trees and saw that anchor splash down. It was a bright moonlight night all over the American continent the night before Columbus slipped into that harbor—did you know that, Carrie? I'm going to tell what that moon shone on— are you listening?"

"Go on. I love it."

Chapter Six

I lay in his arms until it was quite dark and he told me more about his book and how it was not to be an ordinary history at all but a study of Indians and the imprint they have left on our civilization. Then for a few minutes he had nothing to say and then he stirred a little. "What's the matter?"

"I've been thinking, Carrie, just as a sort of peace offering, hadn't I better send some flowers around to my mother?"

"I think that will be fine—as soon as she sends flowers to *me*."

"She sends flowers to—?"

"I'm the bride, after all."

"Oh—that's a different department. What she sends you, that couldn't be just a bunch of flowers, you know, bought at the drop of a hat. But tonight—she's not herself and it will make a difference."

"Can't you order them by phone?"

"I'll have to put a card in. I'll only be a few minutes, and then we'll pick out a nice place to have dinner."

He got his hat and went out, and I was left with this same feeling I had had before, of being sick and forlorn and up against something I didn't understand, and mixed in with it was a sense of helplessness, for I was sure that it wasn't the system, or his Uncle George, or the yachts that was the cause of his trouble, but this same woman he refused to talk about and yet seemed to have on his mind all the time, his mother. And what could I do about her?

The place seemed horribly gloomy then, and I wanted light. I groped all around but couldn't find any of the switches. I began to cry. Then the house phone rang and I went to answer it and couldn't find *that*. Then the phone stopped ringing and in a minute the buzzer sounded. I knew how I had come in, at any rate, so I opened the door. A policeman was standing there. "Carrie Selden Harris?"

"I'm Carrie Harris."

It was the first time I had used my new name and it felt strange, but I tried not to show it to him.

"Warrant for your arrest. I warn you that anything you say in my presence may be used against you—come on."

I asked him to wait, then went to change from my sport outfit, which I still had on, into a dress that seemed more suitable to be arrested in, and then, fumbling around in the dark, I *really* broke down and wept. Why couldn't Grant be there instead of traipsing out to a florist's to send flowers to a woman who hadn't even had the decency to wish him well when he got married? I don't think I could have got dressed at all if the policeman hadn't found a switch and turned it on so that a little light filtered into the bedroom.

I put on my green dress, a green hat and powdered my nose some kind of way and went into the living room. The policeman was a big man, rather young, and looked at me, I thought, in a kind way. "You got any calling to do about bail, something like that, be a good idea to do it from here. Station house phone, sometimes they got a waiting line on it and anyhow you're only allowed one call. Besides, it's pretty high on the wall for you to be talking into."

"Thank you, there's nobody I want to call."

"You got a husband?"

"There's nobody I want to call."

I wouldn't have called Pierre's or waited for Grant to get back if they were going to send me to the electric chair.

■　　■　　■

I had never been in a police station before but I didn't stay there long enough to find out much about it. We rode around in the police car, the officer and I, and it was a battered-looking place with a sergeant behind a big desk, and sure enough, five or six people waiting to use the telephone, which was so high against the wall that everybody had to stand on tiptoe and yell into it. The Sergeant was a fat man who told me I was under arrest on a complaint sworn out by Clara Gruber for embezzlement of union funds, and that if I gave him the required information about myself quickly he might be able to get my case disposed of before the magistrate went home to dinner and at least I would know the amount of bail.

But just as I had finished giving him my name, age and residence, Mr. Holden came striding in and that was the end of it. He said something quickly to the sergeant and then I saw Clara Gruber standing outside the door looking pretty uncomfortable. He beckoned to her and then he, she and the sergeant went into a room where there seemed to be some kind of court in session. When they came out he took my arm and patted it. "It's all over—Clara made a little mistake."

"The money is still in the bank, every cent of it."

"Don't I know it? Come on—the girls are waiting to give you a cheer."

What became of Clara Gruber I don't know, because before I knew it I was in a taxi with him and in a few minutes we were at Reliance Hall. Hundreds of girls were up there holding a big meeting and when he brought me in they all started to yell and applaud and newspaper photographers began clicking flashlights in my eyes and when I got up on the platform the cheering broke out into one long scream. Next thing Mr. Holden was banging for order and a girl was on her feet nominating me for president. Then was when I got into it. I made them a little speech, saying that I still regarded myself as one of them and wanted to keep on being treasurer but that I couldn't be president because I had just got married and might not have the time to give to the duties. However, I never really finished about why I didn't want to be president. As soon as I mentioned my marriage they all broke out again into yells and I realized that why they were cheering for me had nothing to do with the money at all but was really on account of my marrying Grant. I felt warm and friendly and a little weepy, because it meant something after the day I had had to know I had friends, but at the same time I wanted to get out of there, because what they had in mind was a successful Cinderella and I didn't feel that way about it at all and even hated the very idea. Besides, no matter how angry I had been at Grant, I had to get back to him.

Mr. Holden must have guessed what I was thinking, because he banged for order again and made them a little speech saying I had to leave and for them to continue with the reelection of a new president and he would be back. So next day, I found out, they elected a girl by the name of Shirley Silverstein from the Brooklyn restaurant.

■　　　■　　　■

When we got to the street we didn't take a taxi, we went to a little coffee spot around the corner and I ordered bacon and eggs, and Mr. Holden had a cup of coffee. His whole manner changed as soon as we had done our ordering, and he sat there studying me until finally a bitter little smile came over his face. "Well—how does it feel to be rich, envied and socially prominent?"

I could see he was horribly disappointed in me for having, as he thought, engaged in a cold-blooded piece of gold-digging, and I had to exercise control to keep from laughing in wild shrieks. However, I merely said: "Please—I didn't know anything about that until I read the papers."

"I think you're lying."

"I'm not lying."

He lit a cigarette and studied me for a time, then took my hand again. "How's it going?"

"Terribly."

"I wanted you myself."

"Then why didn't you ask me?"

"I made up my mind long ago I would never ask any woman unless I knew she wanted me to—a great deal."

"I thought you meant something else."

"I did. If you didn't want me enough for that I wouldn't want you enough for this."

I felt somehow guilty, as though I ought not to be talking of such things with him at all, so I said nothing. After a moment he went on: "Did you?"

"Why?"

"Because if you did—and do—that other way is still open and this one will be—I mean a wedding, a ring and all the rest of it—as soon as you can get an annulment and forget what you did today. Here we are—if you want me you simply don't go back to him at all."

I thought a long time over that and then I said: "I married the man I wanted."

"You can't get away with it. You aren't of his class—"

"If I hear any more about his class I'll—I'll scream! I'll stand right up here and scream."

"You can scream from now until doomsday and you'll not scream down his class—his class can't be destroyed by screaming. I didn't say he was better than you are—he and a million like him are not worth one girl like you and for all of them together I wouldn't give the powder it would take to blow them to hell. But he is of one class and you are of another. They have never mixed—from the time of Lenin, they have made war, the one upon the other. The trouble with you is, that you're American and you have this stupid illusion of equality. If you came from Europe, as I do, you'd know you're attempting something that can never come to pass, even when a whole caravan of camels march through the eye of a needle. Carrie, you're doomed. Give this foolish thing up, come with me tonight and we'll start out together, two people of a similar kind with some chance of success."

My eggs came then and I ate them, weighing every word he had said. When I was through I replied: "I married the man I want."

■　　　■　　　■

When I got home Grant was sitting in a big chair reading a book, but I could tell from the quick way he was breathing that he had just grabbed the book when he heard my key in the lock. He looked up, then looked back to the book. "Oh, hello, Carrie."

"Hello."

"Been out for a walk? It *is* a beautiful night."

"No—just been getting arrested."

He looked up and stared at me, trying to make up his mind if I was kidding. "...For what?"

"Embezzlement."

He put up his book then and came over to me and I told him briefly what happened, omitting, however, anything about my talk with Mr. Holden. But I was casual about it and when I got through he couldn't seem to think of anything to say. After a few moments he turned away and remarked: "Well—we haven't had that dinner yet."

I went out to the pantry, looked in the icebox and came back. "If you can wait a few minutes you can have exactly what I had."

"Oh—you've eaten?"

"Yes—since you seemed to be more concerned about your mother than about me I thought it advisable to have a little something. I had bacon and eggs. Just have a seat in the breakfast room and yours'll be ready in a little while."

I made him bacon, eggs, buttered bread and coffee, and served them to him there in the dining room. He ate the first two eggs I made him but still looked hungry, so I gave him three more and some extra bacon and poured a glass of milk for him. During all this I don't think three words were spoken, but when he had finished he appeared to be in a more amiable humor. But when I was about through washing the dishes the phone rang and he went in the bedroom to answer it. He came back as I was hanging up the dish towel and his face was white. "Carrie—mother's just been taken to the hospital. I'll have to go over there."

He dashed out of the kitchen and I heard him go into the bedroom. I went in there. He was taking off the smoking jacket he had on when I came home and changing into his street coat. I closed the door and put my back against it. "Where did you say you were going?"

"To mother—they've taken her over to Polyclinic."

"Very well—then I'm going over to the Wakefield Hotel, where a gentleman has just invited me to live with him."

"What?"

"Grant, perhaps you've forgotten. This is our wedding night. You stay with me or I leave."

I opened the door and stepped away from it. "Take your choice. It's her or me."

He stood staring, his face working as though the door were some frightful object. Then he closed it, turned around and stared at me as though I were some frightful object. Then he broke into sobs, fell on the bed and buried his face in the pillow. I turned away, as it made me sick to look at him. Then I snapped the switch and turned out the light.

The next day was one long nightmare of reporters, phone calls, photographers and more reporters. The desk kept sending up stacks of papers as soon as they would come out, and it appeared that his family had now decided to talk and that his uncle, sisters and various relatives all agreed that whom he married was up to Grant. They also agreed, apparently, that while it was his own affair, he had disgraced them pretty thoroughly.

In addition to the interviews there was an item about his mother's being in Polyclinic. After breakfast he went over to see her and to this I made no objection. When he came back I tried to find out what had passed between them, but he was extremely evasive. He pretended to tell me everything, said his mother had assured him that if he loved me there was only one thing for him to do and he had done it and she would have been distressed if he had done anything else. Later I realized that this was probably true. But it was only half true, and Grant, although he tried to conceal it from me, was in more of a turmoil inside, if that was possible, than he had been before. As to the peculiar ways in which she was able to torture him while saying the sweetest things, I cannot explain in a few words, so you will have to let me make this clear when I came to it.

■　　　■　　　■

About four-thirty the house phone rang, and I answered. "Mrs. Bernard Hunt and two other ladies in the lobby, calling on Mr. Harris."

"Will you tell them that Mr. Harris is indisposed at the moment and ask them if they would care to see Mrs. Harris?"

"Just a moment, Mrs. Harris."

By the time Grant had come into the foyer of the apartment where the house phone was, looking very puzzled. "There's nothing the matter with me. Who is it?"

"I think it's your sisters. I'm just giving them a little lesson in manners. Funny, considering their position in society they wouldn't know about such things themselves."

The desk was on the line again, then: "Mrs. Harris?"

"Yes?"

"They'll be right up."

He didn't make any sense out of it, but I pushed him into the bedroom and told him to wait five minutes before he came out. The buzzer sounded then. I counted three slowly and in between kept saying to myself: "Don't talk about the weather!—Don't talk about the weather!—*Don't talk about* the weather!"—Then I opened the door. The three of them were standing there and at once I had a chilly feeling because written all over them, with a big S, was Society. That is, with the exception of the one that turned out to be Mrs. Hunt, who had at least something else besides that. She was not as tall as the other two, who looked like blobby imitations of Grant, and she was a little better-looking and had more shape and zip. I found out later she slightly resembled her mother, and while she was the snootiest of the three, she did seem to have some little spark of humanness, or humor, or whatever you would call it. I tried not to overdo it. I merely looked pleasant, glanced from one to the other, and said: "Mrs. Hunt?"

"I am Mrs. Hunt."

"I'm the new Mrs. Harris, and I think you must be Grant's sister. I've heard him speak of you a number of times."

I held out my hand and she took it, and then introduced the other two, whose names were Elsie and Jane, but I was careful to address them as "Miss Harris." Mrs. Hunt's name turned out to be Ruth, but again I called her Mrs. Hunt. By that time I had got them into the living room and all four of us had said we were so glad to meet each other, which certainly was not true on my part and I don't think it was true on theirs, but I had tried to get them into a position where there was nothing else they could say. I asked them to sit down but at once Mrs. Hunt turned to me and burst out: "But how is poor Grant? My dear, don't tell me it's made him—*really* ill?"

"Oh, he's all right. I'll tell him you're here. I only said he was indisposed so you'd have to call on me instead of him."

That one landed between her eyes just where I aimed it. She blinked, then laid her hand on my arm. "My dear—of course, of *course!* But the papers said something about your being employed, and it didn't occur to me you'd be home."

That one landed between *my* eyes, and I half admired

the fast way in which she had come back at me. But I laughed very gaily and said: "Oh, I'm employed, but we're on strike."

"Oh, how *thrilling!*"

It come like a chorus from all three of them and on that we sat down. I had an awful second when I didn't know what I was going to talk about next, but my eye happened to catch the arrowheads and I began to gabble as fast as I could about the strange Indian collection I had come to live with, and this had a most unexpected result. They all chimed in about how stupid the Indian idea was and how I had to cure Grant of it, and this was not at all what I thought, but I thought it advisable to say it was all so unfamiliar to me I didn't know how I felt about it, and about that time Grant came in.

They all jumped up and I think they had expected to throw their arms around him and offer condolences for the terrible thing that had happened in his life, but as he looked just as big and healthy as ever and merely said hello, without any particular fuss, they sat down again and it was a little flat. So I thought perhaps as I had put them in their places a little, at least to my own satisfaction, I had better set out a little hospitality. I got up and asked: "May I give you some tea?"

"Oh no, my dear, don't even think of it. We'll have to be going in a few minutes anyway. We just stopped by to—"

"—Call on the bride—"

"*Certainly!* But don't even *consider* going to any trouble about us."

That was Mrs. Hunt, and the other two chorused along with her. Grant got up and went out. I did some more babbling about the Indians and in a few minutes he was back, carrying a try with a bottle of Scotch on it, a seltzer siphon, some glasses and a bowl of ice. "Tea is a little out of date, Carrie. I think we'll offer them something more modern."

I got up, took the bottle of Scotch and, as gracefully as I could, pitched it out the window. It seemed the longest time before it broke in the court beside the apartment house. When I heard it crash I turned to him. "That's for correcting my manners. *I* am offering them *tea*."

63

There was a long and extremely dismal silence. Then Mrs. Hunt wriggled in her chair a little. "I guess we take tea."

"I guess you do."

I went out and fixed tea and canapes, which turned out very well, considering what was there to make them with, for I had had no chance to go out and do any marketing at all. Then on the tray I put a bottle of rye and a bottle of brandy and went back in the living room. "Now we have tea, rye and brandy. Which can I give you?"

Mrs. Hunt smiled sourly. "Tea, darling."

But the taller one, Elsie, jumped up and said: "Oh, the hell with it! We've got to say it, so why keep this up? Give me a slug of rye, will you, dear sister-in-law, so I can really fight? Make it double, it'll save time."

The other one, Jane, closed in on the liquor tray and grabbed the bottle. "Two."

"Three," said Mrs. Hunt.

Grant got up. "Oh, hell—let's all have a slug of rye."

So we all began to laugh and they got up and grabbed canapes without waiting for me to pass them, began wolfing them down and grunting that they were pretty good. Then we all had a slug of rye, including myself, a most inadvisable step on my part, as I found out afterwards, for while my restaurant work had made me very expert at serving liquor, I hadn't much experience drinking it. But it all seemed so comical at the time, us hating each other the way we did and at the same time sociably having a drink so we could fight, that I wanted to be a good sport, and so gagged mine down too. Then we all sat down and Grant hooked one knee over his chair and growled: "Well, get at it."

Mrs. Hunt got at it without any further encouragement. She jumped up, charged over to Grant and shook her finger right under his nose. "You big slob! What do you mean by doing a thing like this? Haven't you any regard for us? Haven't you any regard for *her*? Don't you know you've ruined her life?"

That was where I jumped up, for the liquor was reacting on me in a most unexpected way and leading me to do something I practically never do, which is lose my temper. "Who asked you to take up for me? You can confine yourself to your own ruined life or you'll get something that will

64

be a big surprise! I may look small, but I'm perfectly able to throw all three of you down every flight of stairs in this apartment house, and if there's any more of that kind of talk out of you I'll do it."

"Where did you get all that muscle—carrying trays?"

"Yes! And milking cows on my stepfather's farm, and a whole lot of other things you never did."

"Set 'em up in the next alley," said Grant. "Let's all have another drink."

So we all had another drink, and this time when Mrs. Hunt started in, it was on me. "Oh, you needn't be so tough. We've all got to arbitrate, you know."

I wanted to yell at her some more, but all of a sudden it seemed to be too much trouble, and also my tongue felt woolly and thick, so all I said was: "Whass arbitrate?"

"Now we're gett'n somewhere," said Jane, and her tongue seemed to be thick too.

"Arbitrate," said Mrs. Hunt in a very waspish way, "means that for the sake of appearances you have to take us to your bosom and pretend to like us, and we have to take you to our bosoms and pretend we like you, although we don't at all. We'd like that distinctly understood. We think you're terrible."

"Oh, thass all right. I think you're terrible too."

So then everything became extremely cloudy in my mind and yet wholly delightful in a way, because I said the most awful things to them, and they said the most awful things to me, and then we would have another drink and laugh very loudly and start all over again. So then there was a great deal of talk about a cocktail party which Mrs. Hunt would give for me within three or four days because, as she said: a cocktail party practically required no manners at all and I would disgrace them less in that way than at any other form of entertainment she could think of. So I said I thought that was swell and a great deal better than a dinner party would be, because at a dinner party I might get up and begin to serve just from force of habit, and if I ever got hold of a plate of soup I might let her have it in the face. So then Grant said, "Set 'em up in the next alley," which seemed to be about the only remark he could make all afternoon, and Mrs. Hunt said she would give anything to be able to throw soup with such accuracy, and I said it was really no trick at all, that all it needed was something inspirational to aim at. So then Elsie said: "The rye's all gone. Never mind about the soup, redhead, get the cork out of the brandy."

So next thing I knew I was in the bedroom lying down, very sick, and Grant was sitting beside me and they were gone. And next thing I knew, it was very late at night and I was alone there, with my head very clear and a guilty feeling all over me. I got up and went into the living room. Grant was there reading. I went and sat down in his lap and he put his arm around me and ran his fingers through my hair. "How do you feel, Carrie?"

"All right. What happened?"

"Oh—my sisters came and you and I and they had a good Kilkenny fight that cleared the air quite a little."

"What was that about—a cocktail party?"

"Ruth's giving you one. Friday, I believe."

"I don't want to go to her cocktail party."

"I was a little leery of it, but you seemed set on it, so I kept my notions to myself."

"Then I said I'd go?"

"'In Karb's uniform,' were your exact words, 'with a napkin on one arm and a pewter tray under the other.'"

"Tell me something, Grant. Was I drunk?"

"Stinko. And very sweet."

"I've heard about that all my life, being drunk, and here it had to happen to me today, of all times."

"It's all right. I got you to bed."

"Then I'll have to go? To the cocktail party?"

"I'm afraid you're hooked."

Chapter Seven

If I had no very clear recollection about accepting the invitation to the cocktail party the newspapers quickly refreshed my memory. The first of the next day's editions had nothing about it but around the middle of the afternoon some of the people Mrs. Hunt called up must have tipped the reporters off, because when Grant's financial editions came up, there I was again, plastered all over the front pages, with stories of how the family had decided to accept me "on probation," as one paper put it. I had hardly started to read them when the phone rang and it was Mrs. Hunt. She accused me of calling up the papers and giving them the information, and I promptly accused her of the same, so that was how we discovered that it must have been one of the guests who had done it.

Grant was not at home at the time. He was supposed to be on vacation but had gone down to his office in connection with some matter he had to attend to. It threw me into a highly nervous state again and I wanted to call Mrs. Hunt back and tell her I wanted nothing to do with the cocktail party, or her, or any of them, for that matter, but I kept reminding myself that I had to think of Grant and make an earnest effort to adjust myself to a situation that he couldn't very well help. I wanted a chance to think, and as the phone had started ringing again, with reporters asking all sorts of stupid questions, I put on my hat and went out.

I didn't pay any attention to where I was going but next thing I knew I was at Sutton Place. It reminded me of the night Grant and I walked over there and it had all been so simple and gay, so I turned on my heel and started west, toward Broadway. I got as far as Seventh Avenue and turned south toward Times Square. Pretty soon that brought me to the Newsreel Theatre. That seemed to be about the only place I could have any peace in those days, so I bought a ticket and went in.

I was paying very little attention, and had about come to the conclusion that I was going to follow my instincts and not go to the cocktail party, when to my complete astonishment I saw my name appear on the screen with a flash announcement that patrons of the Newsreel Theatre would now get their first glimpse of the Modern Cinderella who had married herself to a million. Then there were shots of the Karb girls on strike and the announcer was rapidly explaining, in a manner very complimentary to me, that while I was now one of the socially elect of New York, I had not renounced my connection with the girls who had followed my leadership in union matters. Then the scene changed to Reliance Hall, with all the girls cheering and me going up on the platform with Mr. Holden, and I certainly had no idea at that time that among the cameras clicking at me was one making moving pictures. Then it changed again to a close shot of me making my little speech to the meeting, and I was surprised how young and unworldly I looked. But at least the green dress was nicely pressed and my hat was on straight and my face was decently powdered, and I thanked my stars I had taken the time to make myself look presentable before going out with the police officer.

When I came to the point where I mentioned my marriage it broke off and there were a lot of quick shots of the girls cheering, and then single shots of a number of girls, one after the other, with the various expressions on their faces, and I did wish they hadn't betrayed so clearly what was in their minds, which was that they wished they had married a rich man too. Then there was a quick shot of Mr. Holden telling them I had to leave, and then here we came, he and I, down past the cameras, he with his arm around me, guiding me through the mob of girls who were trying to take me in their arms or shake hands with me or kiss me. Then it went into some automobile factory stuff, and I got up quickly and went out. The newsboys were still calling my name and I had a feeling there was no place I could go where I would have any peace and once again I was panicky and frightened.

When I got home Grant still hadn't come, so I sat down and waited and when he came in, around six-thirty, he was cold and formal and different from what he had ever been before. He went to the bedroom and after a few minutes I went in there and asked him if he didn't think we had better go out to dinner, and he said he supposed so, and then for a few minutes he stood tying and retying his necktie and nothing was said. Then he turned on me quite savagely. "You said something, I believe, about some man who had invited you to come and live with him."

"Oh, yes. So I did."

"Who is he?"

"Oh, you met him, I believe. A—labor leader."

"Yes, I met him. You and he seem to have been pretty intimate—even after you married me."

"I don't know of any intimacies."

"Why didn't you tell me you went to a union meeting with him?"

"That was in the papers."

"Not all of it. You better go up to the Newsreel Theatre and have a look at yourself."

"Oh, you saw that?"

"I saw it three times—especially the end of it, where he had his arm around you and was patting your hand. And you—you didn't have any objection, did you? Oh, no— you looked up at him every time he did it and—*where did you go with him then?*"

He had his fist doubled up and his eyes were glaring in a most frightening way, but something was singing inside of me and I didn't care whether he hit me or not. So I switched my hips as impudently as I could and said: "I went to dinner."

He took me by the shoulders and shook me and then our lips met and everything went swimming around and we lost all track of time until it was quite late. Then we were very near to each other and in love and I told him I had just acted that way because I liked to see him jealous. Then we went to dinner and I knew then that I wouldn't be able to tell him I had decided not to go to the cocktail party.

■   ■   ■

I made all preparations for this horrible event as carefully as I could and yet I became more and more nervous as Friday approached. I went to Miss Eubanks, the saleslady who had been so helpful to me before, and let myself be guided by her advice. She suggested two outfits, one in case the summer weather held, and another in case it should turn cold or rainy or both. This I thought a good idea, and for the first I picked out a chartreuse green. It was very expensive, but Miss Eubanks insisted that my costume should be very simple and reminded me that simplicity is only to be found in well-made clothes. This I knew to be true, so I took it, and she went with me to the hat department and I picked out a very lovely hat to go with it. It was another shade of green, and then we bought bronze shoes. She kept cautioning me not to get anything that looked like an ensemble. "You want to be dressed—not dressed up." For the other outfit she suggested a suit and I picked out a steel blue which went very well with my hair, brown suede hat and brown shoes. She hesitated about letting me wear a suit that was ready-made, but finally concluded that with my figure, since it was very well tailored, it would be all right. Then she had me buy proper handbags, stockings and all accessories, and I paid with my personal check. It made quite a dent in my savings, but for some reason I wanted to appear in *my* things and not things that Grant had bought me. And that was why I went for them alone too, as I didn't want to feel or have him or *anybody* feel that I had needed any coaching from him.

Friday was a beautiful day, with just a touch of fall in the air, and he was so delighted with the way I looked in the chartreuse dress that I was almost glad I was going, and yet a nervous feeling kept spreading from the pit of my stomach until, as four-thirty approached, I wasn't sure whether I would be able to go through with it or not. About a quarter after four he suddenly said: "Let's walk, it's not far."

"Oh, yes—let's." Because I thought I would die if I had to sit and watch the El posts go by in a taxi.

"Then let's start now."

"I'm ready."

So we walked, and it did take a little of the nervousness out of me. We went over and turned up Park Avenue. Grant had got a hair-cut in the morning, quite unusual for him, and had on a dark brown suit and a new fall hat and carried a stick. I knew I looked very well, and for a few minutes I was very proud to be swinging along with him up Park Avenue, with people turning to look and a sense of being somebody.

The house was on Sixty-first Street between Park and Madison, and it was a whole house, not just an apartment. We were let in by a house-man who spoke to Grant and bowed to me. We then went upstairs to a large living room and Mrs. Hunt came in and we sat around talking as though we had never called each other names. We were ahead of the crowd, as she had asked us to be, and it was all very quiet and casual. Then Elsie and Jane arrived and joined in the discussion and you would hardly have known they were giving any party at all. I really didn't like Mrs. Hunt, or any of them, but I caught the point and remembered it: Never make a fuss about your hospitality, as so many people I had known were so prone to do. Then Mr. Hunt came in. He had just left his office and disappeared for a little while to dress, but he stopped long enough to shake hands with me and I caught him eyeing me sharply and, I thought, in a not unfriendly way. He was considerably older than Mrs. Hunt, who was younger than Grant, as were the other two girls, but even so he couldn't have been more than thirty-five, and was tall and rather good-looking. When he came down again he had on a short black coat and gray trousers, and I had a sudden reminder that, in spite of the pleasant casualness of the preliminaries, what I had to go through with would be, for me at any rate, very formidable indeed.

Then the guests began to arrive and they were being introduced to me very rapidly and I must say Mrs. Hunt was very graceful and considerate about it and made it seem that everything was in my honor and I almost felt I was welcome. So in a few minutes I was faced with what worried me most of all, which was what to talk about. Once more I had drilled it into myself: *"Don't talk about the weather."* But what else did I know to talk about? This had given me several bad nights, for I try to be honest with myself, and after a great deal of restless tossing around I had come to the realization that I didn't *know* anything to talk about. I had never read any books or heard any music or seen any pictures or done any traveling. Of what is called culture I had none whatever. My world had been limited to my work, my savings and the few people I had come in contact with, and that was all I ever talked about with other girls of my kind from morning until night. But certainly I couldn't begin complaining about the slowness of Karb's counterman to these people, or criticize the way the cooks neglected to break the soft-boiled eggs, so the waitress had to do it. For Grant's sake I had to give some kind of account of myself, and I stood there shaking hands, badly frightened as to what it was going to be, when suddenly an idea hit me.

I began telling them about the strike. Luck was with me, for all of them became excited and wanted to hear about it, and so the ice was broken in two ways. I had found something that interested them and that I knew enough about not to make a fool of myself in discussing it, and also it relieved them of any embarrassment they may have felt about mentioning my occupation, and I breathed much easier. When another houseman came with a tray of cocktails I took one and sipped it a little so I could laugh and seem to be having a good time, but I was careful of the amount I drank, for I didn't want any repetition of what had happened before. One thing helped me a great deal. In my work as a waitress I had trained myself to remember people's names and use them in speaking to them, as that is the way to get regular customers. So it was no trouble for me to keep all the names straight, even after fifty or sixty people had arrived, and this greatly astonished Mrs. Hunt. I thought it advisable not to tell her how I became so name-conscious, but I could see that she was favorably impressed and also was breathing much easier.

■   ■   ■

This went on for about an hour and I managed fairly well, for when the strike ran thin one of them would usually say something which permitted me to let *them* take the lead and I fell back on something which has stood me in great stead before, especially with talkative customers. I professed to be greatly interested, which in a way I was, and asked a lot of eager questions, so that they would do the talking for a little while.

I must have been acquitting myself quite creditably, because Mr. Hunt drifted by one time, leaned close to me and mumbled in my ear: "You're doing fine."

I had got separated from Grant, as I wanted to be, since I shouldn't appear a clinging vine that he had to look out for, and of course Mrs. Hunt was too busy to be paying much attention to me anymore. Then two or three women who were talking to me suddenly stopped what they were saying and glanced over my shoulder toward the entrance from the outer hall. I became aware that a strained hush had fallen over the room. I turned around and there, standing with Mrs. Hunt, was one of the most beautiful women I had ever seen. She didn't appear to be over thirty-eight, she was even smaller than I am, with a lovely figure and beautiful high color in her cheeks that you could tell at once was natural. Her hair was blonde but shot slightly with gold so it was very brilliant. Her eyes were a peculiarly vivid green which I could see even from where I was. She had on the simplest summer dress, black with a design in it, and yet with her figure you could hardly take your eyes off it. She seemed to radiate charm and friendliness, and I was still staring at her when Mrs. Hunt came over to me. Her face was drawn and nervous and she didn't quite look me in the eye when she spoke. "Don't say I did this to you. She wasn't even invited. So come on. But I can tell you this much. The worst you can possibly imagine can't be as bad as it's really going to be."

"Who is it?"

"Mother."

It seemed impossible that one so young could be Grant's mother, but I later found out she had been married at seventeen and that Grant came along as soon as the law allowed. But in spite of my surprise a chill began to creep up my backbone. I took a deep breath and we crossed the room.

Chapter Eight

We had no sooner done so than I discovered that the warm friendliness was all on the outside, with none on the inside whatever. She had shaken hands with some woman and stood there talking about a Commander in the Navy and the funny way he used to kick the goals when he was a midshipman at Annapolis, keeping Mrs. Hunt and me waiting and never looking at us at all. Even the woman was getting uncomfortable and Mrs. Hunt was growing more irritated by the second. Suddenly she cut in sharply:

"Mother! . . . If you can interrupt that fascinating discourse on the drop kicks long enough—"

"Place kicks, dear. Not drop kicks."

"They'll be just plain shin kicks if I hear any more about them—I'd like to present Granny's new bride, the young Mrs. Harris."

Mrs. Harris looked at me then and her eyes seemed to shrink into two pieces of hard green glass. She opened her arms, drew me to her and spoke in a voice that fairly throbbed with emotion: "Darling! Oh, I've been looking forward *so* much to meeting you! Every day I made up my mind to pay you a visit but I've been so ill—really, you have no idea. Will you overlook it—can you bring yourself to forgive me?"

She didn't look ill and I didn't believe she cared whether I forgave her or not, but I thought if she was going to be hypocritical I might as well too, so I made my voice sound as gushy as I could and said: "And I too, Mrs. Harris! I so wanted to call at the hospital the moment I heard you were there but I wasn't sure you would like it, because so few of us look well in hospitals, do we?"

This dirty crack seemed to surprise her greatly but nothing like as much as it surprised me, so we stood grinning at each other, our arms intertwined, and for a moment neither of us had any more to say. Then a servant came up with a tray of cocktails and she stood there at her favorite trick of making everybody wait. This time it was while she decided what kind of cocktail she wanted. There were Martinis, Manhattans and side-cars on the tray, but of course, after changing her mind for five minutes she had to have an old-fashioned and, just to make it good and complicated, it had to be an old-fashioned made with Scotch. I wanted to get away from her, so, having been audacious about my occupation once with some success, I thought I would try it again and appear to be exceedingly nice to her while at the same time removing myself from where she was. I said: "Oh, Mrs. Harris, do let me make you one. I know exactly how you want it and I'm an expert at old-fashioneds with Scotch—I used to make so many when I was a waitress at the Solon Cocktail Bar."

Her eyes opened wide, as though this was the most heavenly idea she had ever heard in her life. "Oh, darling— *would* you?" Then she looked around at everybody and exclaimed: "Isn't that marvelous? Think of being an expert!" And then to me again: "There's so much that you'll have to teach me!"

By that time the big table at one side of the room had been converted into a sort of bar and one of the housemen was mixing drinks while the other passed them around. But of course some of the guests were standing around getting their drinks direct from the bar, so when I stepped over, there was quite a gallery, some of them rather friendly toward me. An old-fashioned with Scotch was nothing new to me, so I put it together very quickly, and when I got through two or three men laughed and gave me a little hand. When I went over with it to Mrs. Harris she was again talking about place kicks, and kept me standing there, glass in my hand. But as though to be very friendly, she raised her hand and without looking around put it on my arm. There was an exclamation from somebody and there went the cocktail all over her dress, and the orange, cherry and ice all over the floor.

I had served rush orders in a crowded cocktail bar with drunks elbowing me from every side and I assure you it is almost impossible to make me drop anything or do something clumsy like spilling a cocktail. That grip on my arm was like iron and it was deliberate. But there was nothing for me to do but get down and begin dabbing at her dress with my handkerchief, then call for a napkin and dry her off as best I could. All that time she talked a mile a minute, loudly proclaiming that it was all her fault, and that I mustn't mind, as the dress was an old rag anyhow, but there I was, stooped in front of her, making a holy show of myself when I wanted to be at my best.

It was Mr. Hunt who rescued me. He lifted me to my feet, patted my arm and drew me aside. Then for the first time Mrs. Harris became shrill. "But, Bernie, I'm wringing wet! Just look at my dress!"

"That's what we have dry cleaners for."

"And that's what we have such dresses for." It was Mrs. Hunt who said this, very grimly. "That's the third cocktail that's been spilled on it this year. Or was it a Tom *Collins* last time?"

Mrs. Harris' answer to this was to make a speech in which she said she didn't know what people were coming to, the ill-bred way they got drunk and spilled drinks all over her, but Mrs. Hunt took me to another part of the room and that seemed to be the end of it. She gave me a cocktail and mumbled: "Don't worry about her dress. It's fast color, quick-drying crepe, bought especially to have cocktails spilled on it and get women down on their knees and make them feel foolish. You behaved very well and you needn't give it a thought."

The man who had been passing cocktails came up just then and said: "She's here, Mrs. Hunt."

"Oh. Then you'd better take out some of those glasses and tell her to wash them up as quickly as she can, but don't wait for her to get through with them. You come back to keep things moving here, and have her bring them in as soon as they're ready."

"Yes, Mrs. Hunt."

She turned to me. "I did something I rarely do. I borrowed a maid from Mrs. Norris, but of course the children had to be taken to the park as usual and she has only now arrived—when it's almost all over."

"It's been going beautifully."

"It's been going somehow, but I hate that clutter of used glasses at a cocktail party. The very idea that I might have been drinking out of somebody else's glass makes *me* squirm, and I don't see why my guests should feel differently."

It seemed like a trifling thing at the time but only too often in the weeks that followed I wished bitterly that one of the children had got lost in the park so that maid never arrived.

■　　■　　■

Mr. Hunt had disappeared, and now came up from downstairs and hurried over to his wife. "What do we do now?"

"What is it, Bernie?"

"The reporters and photographers. They're lined up outside of the house three deep trying to get in and Gus is having a hard time to keep them out."

"You'd better call an officer."

He thought a moment, then said: "I wonder..."

She looked at him very intently and he rubbed his chin and thought a few moments. Then he said; "If that angelic mother of yours could be induced to pose for a few pictures with Grant and Carrie I have an idea this thing could be washed up right now."

"That'll never work."

"What the hell? Are you going to keep it up forever? She's married to him, she's been a perfectly delightful guest, she's all right. The thing to do is to tap this newspaper stuff and let some of the pressure off. Having all three of their pictures taken will turn the trick and then these headlines will die off so fast it'll amaze you."

Mrs. Hunt rather absent-mindedly put her arm around me and shook her head. "I'm not thinking about her. She's been fine, and I take back all I said about her and—" with a little pat to me—"*to* her. But you can't trust mother. She'll *pull* something—"

"What can she pull?"

"She can pull nonsense you and I could never think of, and I'm warning you, you may be starting something that'll be dreadful before you get through with it."

"In these things I have a gift."

He went over to Mrs. Harris, who by now had decided to be in a gay mood again, and said something to her. She turned and came over to me, her arms outstretched, which seemed to be her regular way of approaching anybody. "But, darling, I'd simply *love* to. Why, of course—I had no idea the photographers were out there or I would have suggested it myself."

So Mr. Hunt went downstairs and next thing the photographers and reporters were trooping in, all very noisy and impudent, and a buzz of excited talk was going around the room and Mr. Hunt was asking everybody to stand back a little to give the photographers a chance. So then Grant came over and put his arm around his mother and had tears in his eyes and I didn't believe for a second that she was as sweet as she pretended to be, but I was like Mr. Hunt: even if she didn't like me, having the picture taken would probably end all these terrible things in the newspapers, because if she accepted me, at any rate publicly, there couldn't be much left for the newspapers to say.

So we all lined up. At first the photographers wanted me in the middle, then they changed their minds and put Mrs. Harris in the middle, and then finally they decided it would be better with Grant in the middle, his arm around each of us. So then they told us to smile and yelled "hold it," and I was standing there with the grin pasted patiently on my face, when all of a sudden there was the most awful crash and everybody jumped and looked around.

■   ■   ■

It seemed a year before my mind could comprehend that who I was looking at was Lula Schultz, the girl who had shared the room with me at the Hotel Hutton and who had disappeared after we had the big quarrel over my staying out with Grant. She was the maid who had arrived late, and I found out later that after she quit her job at Karb's she had taken a place as a servant with Mrs. Norris. However, I didn't know any of that then, and all I was aware of was the mess on the floor and Lula staring at me and all the rest of them staring at the two of us. Then a reporter seemed to sense something, for he held up his hand to the photographers and for a moment there was absolute silence. Then Lula contributed her brilliant remark: "Well, for crying out loud, Carrie, where did you come from?"

Then the photographers woke up and for a minute or more it was like a madhouse, with the cameras clicking first at Lula, standing there with the tray, the glasses all over the floor in front of her, then at me, then at Mrs. Harris and Grant, and it later turned out that one or two of them had got over into a corner to shoot the whole scene. All while they were taking pictures they were yelling at us in the most disrespectful way. Then Mrs. Hunt tried to take command and get Lula out of there and the mess cleared away, but all she would do was stand and gape and gabble at me that she seen all about it in the papers but she hoped she'd drop dead if she had any idea it was the same party she had been sent over to work at. She spoke terrible grammar, which is something I have always tried to avoid.

I was furious enough to break the tray over her head, but there was only one thing for me to do and I gritted my teeth and did it. I went over and shook hands with her as calmly as though it were nothing at all. That was when Mrs. Harris screeched: "Isn't she simply a *dear!* And mustn't she be thrilled! Imagine—an old friend from the slums and meeting her here! It's such a small world!"

78

． ■ ．

Somehow, by asking a number of his friends to help and practically using main force, Mr. Hunt got the photographers and reporters out and Mrs. Hunt must have dealt with Lula for she wasn't there any more, and then for fifteen or twenty minutes everybody stood around and talked about it, except that when I approached they hurriedly began to talk about something else. Then they all went, shaking hands with me very hurriedly, and then I found myself alone in the living room, as Grant, his three sisters and his mother having gone somewhere else. But in a moment Mr. Hunt came in, made two highballs and said: "Let's go in here—it's not so public."

He took me into a small library and closed the door. We sat down and sipped our drinks and he kept rubbing the moisture on his glass with his thumb. Then he said: "I'm not sure, but I think that sinks you."

"You mean Lula?"

"Couldn't you have pretended it was a case of mistaken identity or something?"

"If I were sick or needed somebody she's the one person on earth that I could call on."

"I suppose there was nothing else you could do, but if you think the noble Grant is going to take a broad attitude toward it, you're very optimistic."

"Grant is not a complete fool."

"No, but he's a complete snob, and that's serious."

"I haven't seen any signs of it."

"Did you ever hear of the silver cord?"

"What's that?"

"An intangible but terrible bond, that sometimes exists between mother and son, and invariably spells trouble for them both. Not one thing about Grant is on the up-and-up except his interest in Indians. His phony radicalism, his rebellion against Uncle George, his nutty talk about breaking the system, and all the rest of it merely represent his feeble effort to break the silver cord, and whether he can do it I wouldn't like to say. But I know this much: Lula will give Mama a club over him that he'll feel from morning to night.

And don't make any mistake about it: Grant is the worst snob of the lot."

"He married me. That doesn't look much like a snob."

"Masochism."

"...*What* did you say?"

"Torturing himself, going out in the back yard and eating worms so Mama will feel ashamed of herself, for trying to make him marry Muriel."

"Why, by the way, *did* she try to make him do that?"

"Money, partly. With those two fortunes blended many things would be possible. But mainly because Muriel is a dull cluck of a girl that Mama wouldn't have to be jealous of that Grant hates. The silver cord binds two ways."

"Why does she oppose the Indians?"

"Sadism."

"You're using words I'm not familiar with."

"She also likes to torture him, and she's not done yet."

"What else can she do?"

"One thing she can do is begin trotting round with some man. That's what she usually does, and when she starts it this time I predict Grant will go simply insane. I don't think you quite understand this yet. It's not pretty. It's unnatural, unhealthy and tragic. But it's what you're up against."

"You mean—she wants to make him jealous as though she were some girl he was in love with—or that was in love with him?"

"Exactly. Except that it's a love that can never get anywhere. If you ask me, Mama has some strange youth complex. I think she resents Grant—why Grant and not the other three I can't explain, except that he came first— because he compelled her to become a woman instead of the seventeen-year-old girl that she instinctively wants to be. When he arrived, that was the end of her youth. But it doesn't help any that her youth is still with her, so far as her appearance goes, and so is a habitual interest in men and a trained technique at getting them. As to her morals, I prefer not to speak. Grant had the misfortune to be born to a woman who could still be his sweetheart, and it's the blight of his life."

I didn't feel depressed or hysterical as I had felt before in these last few days. I merely felt cold and weak from encountering things that I didn't understand. Still, I heard myself say: "Well—what am I going to do about it?"

"Perhaps there's nothing you can do about it. Reckoning conditions of the track, form of the starters and confidential information from the paddock, I would rate your chances at about one to ninety-nine. If it were myself, I think I'd scratch my entry and be done with it. Of course you may feel differently."

To that I made no reply. He sipped his drink, then came over to me, sat on the arm of my chair and turned my face up to him. "I like you, for some reason. I could see your head working in there this afternoon. You played your cards well and if there's one thing I enjoy it's seeing somebody lead into dummy, finesse through trouble and win through a grand slam. But you haven't got the cards, that's all. I'm on your side, and if there's anything I can do you can call on me. But what I really think is: You're sunk."

■   ■   ■

When we went back in the living room everybody except Grant had gone and he had his hat and stick and was waiting for me. I thanked Mrs. Hunt and she said it had been a pleasure, but her eyes had the same glassy look I had seen in her mother's and I knew that her little flurry of friendliness was over and that so far as she was concerned the whole thing had been a fiasco that would not be repeated.

Grant and I walked down Madison a few blocks, then crossed over and had dinner at a place on Fifty-fifth Street. There would be long silences and then he would talk feverishly about things like the Army Air Force and the new planes they were building. It was well after eight when we left the Hunts and it must have been ten o'clock when we got through dinner. We walked down Fifth Avenue to Fifty-fourth Street, then over toward the apartment. As we crossed Third Avenue a truck was unloading tabloids at a newsstand. I stopped and bought one and there, sure enough, was the first of those terrible pictures that came out showing Lula at the cocktail party with numbers all over it and down at the bottom the names, corresponding to the numbers, of all the prominent people who were present. We started along again but as we went I was looking at the paper. Suddenly he stopped, snatched the paper out of my hand and threw it down on the pavement. He ran toward it and kicked it, then kicked it again and again until it was just a litter of pages flying all over the street. Then he stood there panting, and I knew that everything Mr. Hunt had said was true. He hated that picture, hated Lula and I think at that moment hated me. In spite of all his fine talk he was really what money, education and family had made him, a snob who had no respect for what my life had made me. A terrible sense of helpless pain swept over me, of being hurt more than I knew I could be hurt, and it was then that I knew how much I loved him and how desperately I had to fight, even if the chances were one to ninety-nine against me.

Part Three:
THE SNAKE

Chapter Nine

From then on Grant and I were almost strangers to each other. There were times when we forgot everything else and were terribly close, but they were merely occasional interludes in what was beginning to feel like the unreal dreams one has in a fever. The newspapers were only incidental so far as I was concerned. What made it so terrible was Grant and the grim, hunted look he had all the time, and especially when he came back to the apartment after going out for a little while, and I knew he had seen his family or his friends or somebody and had felt compromised and embarrassed in talking with them.

However, the worst was yet to come, for I wasn't done yet with Lula Schultz. On the Monday after the cocktail party, about ten o'clock in the morning, a few minutes after Grant had gone down to his office to pick up his mail, she had shown up. The desk phoned in a very queer way that a woman was in the lobby to see me. I told them to send her up and when I opened the door there she was, a straw suitcase in one hand and looking like something that had come out of a bread line. Her eyes were red, her face pasty, her clothes all bedraggled, and when she saw me she swayed as though she were about to fall. I caught her and brought her inside, then hastily went out and took in the suitcase, for the elevator man was still there, staring as though he could hardly believe his eyes. When I got outside she was half lying on the big sofa and began to talk in her usual rough and ungrammatical way. "I hope I may drop dead, Carrie, I never meant to ask anything off you. I wasn't going to bother you, but I couldn't pass out right in Central Park, could I? Being drug down to Bellevue in a police car wouldn't do you no good. Soon as I give my name them papers would have started in on you all over again. I know 'em. They don't never give you no break."

"Central Park? What are you talking about?"

"A wooden bench, Carrie. With a bum on one end of it and me on the other, and newspapers in the middle. Where I spent last night and the night before—without room service. They didn't send up no meals."

"You slept on a park bench?"

"I didn't do very good after I left my happy home in Hutton. Took that job minding babies till I could find something better, but a fat chance I could hold that after I dropped them canapes all over the floor. Sweetheart, I'm telling you, Lady Norris was a little annoyed. I got fired fast, but not so fast I didn't get a sweet bawling out. Carrie, you'd of died laughing if you'd heard what *I* told *her*. Then was when I begun to live in the park."

"Didn't you get paid off?" I asked this in all sincerity, for it did seem peculiar that she had to live in the park immediately after getting her money. As to how this came about I was to find out much more later, but in view of her exhausted condition, or what at any rate *appeared* to be her exhausted condition, I didn't press her too hard when she became, as I thought, extremely vague.

"Circumstances, Carrie—just circumstances. They drive me nuts. Say, you got something to eat in the house? My stomach is a little empty, if you know what I mean."

I got her a glass of milk, for I thought if she hadn't eaten in forty-eight hours, as seemed to be the case, she had better be a little careful about how she resumed her relations with food. Then I said something about making her some coffee and went out in the kitchen again and put the water on to heat, but what I was really doing was getting off by myself for a few minutes so I could think what I was going to do with her. I had got to the point of calculating that if I jumped in a taxi and dashed over to the bank very quickly I could draw $50, give it to her and get her out of there before Grant came home. I even improved on this by deciding I would take her to the bank with me and then I wouldn't risk her being there if he got home while I was gone.

But then something in me began to rebel. In the first place,

I felt that if it had been *I* who had spent two nights in a park and *she* who was living in a comfortable apartment, there would be no question of getting me out of there at all. I would be taken in simply as a matter of course, and in spite of the complicated trick that she was playing on me, as it later turned out, I still believe that this much, at least, she would have done for me. And in the second place, as I pointed out to Mr. Hunt, Lula was the one person, aside from Mr. Holden, perhaps, who had meant something to me before I married Grant, and in some instinctive way I knew that I must not give her up. I stood looking out into the bright sunlight, waiting for the water to boil, and there popped into a mind a recollection of the big waves racing past the boat while the sun was still shining that afternoon on the Sound, and I had the same tingling sensation that a storm was coming up. But this time, whether there would be a buoy to grab I wasn't at all sure.

■　　　■　　　■

In addition to the coffee I made Lula soft-boiled eggs and toast and she began gobbling them down there in the living room. Later, in some connection, I learned that people who have not eaten for some time are not at all hungry and have to force themselves to eat. But at the time Lula's appetite seemed wholly natural, and I left her there for a while to do what I had to do.

There was a den in the living room. But there was a cot in there and this I made up with clean sheets, pillow cases and blankets. Among the things stored in there were a bundle of Navajo blankets. I cut the string on this and spread a couple of them on the floor so the room wouldn't feel so bare. The rest of them, as well as the other things, I piled as neatly as I could in one corner of the room, draped a sheet over them and called Lula. She came in and I went into the living room and got her suitcase. When I came back she had lifted the sheet and was peeping at the Indian things. But she dropped it when she saw me and I pretended not to notice. Then I suggested that she go to bed and get some sleep. She didn't want to, but I insisted and helped her undress. She had no clean pajamas in her suitcase but I got a suit of my own and pretty soon I had her tucked in. I pulled the shade to keep the sun out of her eyes and went in the living room to wait for Grant. It was nearly one o'clock when he came in and at once suggested that we go out somewhere for lunch. I still had this tingling sensation all over me, and my mouth felt dry and hot, because I knew I had to tell him about Lula, and yet I couldn't seem to begin. So I said all right but I wasn't hungry yet, and he went in the bedroom.

When he came out he lit a cigarette, inhaled it nervously three or four times, then squashed it out and looked at me. "May I make a request?"

"Certainly."

"Well—there are certain little decencies around an apartment I like to observe. I realize that women have their own ways of doing things. Just the same—damn it, this is what I'm trying to say: do you mind in the future not using the bathroom for a laundry?"

I got up and went into the bathroom. It was the worst mess I had ever seen in my life, even worse than our bathroom at the Hutton used to be on the infrequent occasions when Lula had decided that her things were too dirty to wear any more and that she had to wash them. She had tied two or three strings across the room and they were full of stockings, brassieres, and everything else imaginable. The beautiful porcelain hand-basin was full of rings, dirt and soap where she hadn't washed it out properly after she got done, and even the bathtub was draped with more of her things drying, such as girdles. And in addition to that, you could hardly breathe for the horrible stench of laundry drying.

I jerked down the strings, gathered everything up into one armful and went in to where she was lying in bed smoking a cigarette. I dumped the whole wet pile over her head, turned on my heel and walked out. Then I went back in the living room.

I sat down, closed my eyes and tried to begin. But all I could say was: "They weren't my things."

"Then whose were they?"

"...Lula's."

"Who is Lula?"

"The maid at the cocktail party."

I think I have told you that Grant is very heavily sunburned and under that there is usually a touch of his mother's high color. As he looked at me and realized the implication of what I had said I saw every bit of the color slowly leave his face until it was like gray chalk. "...You mean she's here?"

"She got fired. She—had no place to stay. I took her in."

"I—don't *want* her here."

"Neither do I."

"Then what did you let her in for?"

"I had to."

"Why?"

"She would have done the same for me."

"But good God, we can't have her here. Why—I won't have it! I—"

"I *will* have it."

"You—? *You'll* have it?"

"I invited her in. It's my home."

Afterwards I liked to remember that Grant did not get excited when I told him that or say that it was *his* home and I had only recently been brought into it, or anything like that. In these trying days Grant constantly seemed like a weak, spineless creature and helpless in the hands of his mother for reasons that he could not at the time help. But meanness was never a part of him. There was a generosity in him that I could always count on and this was one reason why, even when I had the most contempt for him, some little part of me was always proud of him and confident that he would never strike at me in some unfair way.

"I thought it was *our* home."

That touched me and I started to cry. He bounded over, put his arms around me and pulled me close to him. "What have you got that bum here for, Carrie? We can't have her come between us! To hell with her! We—"

I pushed him away and stood up. More than anything I wanted to be in his arms and getting myself clear left me weak and trembling. But I drove myself to say what I had to say. "Grant!"

"Yes, Carrie, what is it?"

"That girl has to stay here."

"All right, Carrie. I don't get it, it seems to me a little money would dispose of her case a whole lot better, but if you say she stays she stays. But—keep her out of sight, will you? I don't want to see her. I—"

"I will not keep her out of sight."

"I warn you, Carrie, you had better keep her away from me or I won't be responsible for what I—"

"You are going to accept her."

"That—*servant girl?*"

"That servant girl is going to live with us until she can find some other place, she is going to eat with us—"

"With *you*. You can count me out."

"With *us!*"

I fairly screamed it. Understand, I wasn't saying exactly what I meant. Because by this time I had made up my mind that as soon as he accepted Lula, Lula was going out the door as fast as her legs would carry her, and her wet wash along with her. But I was not going to tell him this until I had gained my point.

When I yelled at him he lit another cigarette, sat down and waited a few moments, evidently to regain some sort of calm. Then he looked at me, smiled in what was meant to be a friendly way, and said: "There's something back of this, Carrie. All right—here I am. I'm acting reasonably, I hope. I'm not trying to stir up a fight. Now will you tell me what it is? In words of one syllable, so I understand it all?"

"Yes."

"All right, then, shoot."

"Grant, I'm calm too—if you'll overlook that little outbreak just now—and I'm not trying to stir up a fight either. This is what lies back of it. You think you're objecting to Lula. That's not it. You're really objecting to me."

"Why, that's ridiculous."

"You think it is, but it isn't. Grant, Lula is my friend. She's almost the only friend I've got. I admit she's not much of a friend. I wish she was different. I bitterly wish she was different. But she's not different. Lula is the world I came from. Perhaps it's not much of a world, I don't know. But it was my world and I can't change it. The trouble with you is, you're trying to pretend I was not part of that world at all. You're trying to convince yourself that in some ways I was an exception, that I didn't really belong in that world. Well, I'm an exception. I've got more gump than most girls in that world have got and I've found out by now that I've got more brains. I do better than they do. I make more money and I have more ambition. But whether I'm an exception or not, I was a part of that world and I'm still part of it. If it wasn't for you, money would take care of Lula's case, and I have money, anyhow, a little bit, and I would be willing to take care of it. But I can't keep you out of it. As you say, there you are, and if you don't accept Lula you don't accept me. I have done my best to accept your friends, to say nothing of your family. I have conquered my pride, eaten their bread and drunk their liquor, even when they told me I wasn't welcome. You are going to do the same. When you sit down to the table and eat dinner with me and Lula Schultz, then I'll know that it's not true, some of the things that people say about you."

"What do people say about me?"

"...That was a slip. I shouldn't mention things that have been said about you, and I'm sorry."

"I asked what they said about me."

"They say you're a snob."

"All right. Perhaps I am."

"I don't really care what you are, Grant. I'm a snob, too, in a way. I'm terribly conceited and always thinking I'm more capable than other people and—I don't care about that either. You can be what you are and I'll not complain. But—*you'll have to accept me*. I'll take no less."

"I accept you but I will not accept this—Lula. Whatever her name is."

"Grant, whenever I have something difficult I always try to think it over a little before I come to a decision. Will you do that much for me?"

He came over, put his arms around me again and stood with me a long time, giving me little pats on the arm. "I'll think it over, Carrie. But I know in advance the decision I'll come to. I'll not accept Lula."

■　　　■　　　■

So he didn't accept her, and she stayed on and on and on. Every afternoon she would go out on the pretense of seeking work but would be back by five-thirty in time for dinner, for she always seemed to have a big appetite. But Grant hardly ever saw her. He left the apartment long before she got up, around nine o'clock most mornings, and didn't come home until eleven or twelve at night.

Two or three days of this was bad enough, but when the story of my life began to run in one of the tabloids it was even worse. They had everything in there, from the orphan asylum to my girlhood on the farm, to my job as a waitress in Nyack, but they had it all garbled up, and although it was written in a way as to seem friendly to me, it made your skin crawl, the things they put in. It was not signed, so it was impossible to tell who was writing it. The night after it started when Grant came home, I tried to get him to do something about it as it seemed to me they had no right to print my life story unless I gave my consent. But he merely shrugged his shoulders and said it didn't make any difference. Next day I called Mr. Hunt and he said he would consult a lawyer. But the next morning when he called me back, he said the lawyer had told him they did have the right, provided the story was not malicious, and that while I could seek an injunction, if I wanted to, the probability was that I wouldn't be successful.

I told him never mind, and the horrible story kept running and running, and when it got to the point of my marriage with Grant it revealed shockingly intimate details of our life together, until I thought I would go insane from reading it. Yet all I could do was sit every morning and every evening with Lula and listen to her gabble about how badly Grant treated me and what she would do if she were in my place.

■　　　■　　　■

One day around lunch time Grant came in with his mother. She made herself very agreeable, and I said nothing to indicate there had been any unpleasantness between us. I remembered that she liked an old-fashioned with Scotch, got out the tray and made her one, gave Grant a rye highball, and waited for her to say what she wanted. She came to the point very quickly. Smiling at me so that her eyes didn't look like glass at all, she said: "I hear a little situation has developed in connection with the young lady who is staying here."

My first impulse was to look surprised and act as though I couldn't imagine what situation she meant, but on second thought I decided that frankness would probably be the better policy. So I said: "Yes, I'm afraid that's true."

"You feel some sense of loyalty to the girl, Grant tells me."

"I feel some sense of that, and I also feel that she represents something I have to make an issue over with Grant. If I back down on Lula I've lost everything. I've renounced what I was, I can't change myself into something else, and that will leave me being exactly nothing at all. I won't be that."

"In your place I wouldn't either."

She smiled then and turned to Waldo. "It's just as I told you—a question of pride. Not stubbornness, not stupidity, not capriciousness. It's pride, pure and simple, and you have to respect it."

"I respect it, but I don't respect Lula."

She sipped her cocktail, smiled at me again and, although I knew I couldn't for a second trust her, I felt myself yielding to the charm she could turn on when she wanted. "May I call you Carrie?"

"Certainly, Mrs. Harris."

"Then, Carrie, why don't you let me step in with a plan that might relieve the whole difficulty?"

"I would be delighted if you could."

"The girl, as I understand it, is out of work. Very well, then I'll give her a job."

I didn't know what to say about this. It didn't meet the issue I had spoken of, and yet I was so sick of Lula and so miserable about the point I had come to with Grant, that I only wished to wash my hands of the whole mess and start over again, if that was possible. She must have sensed what was in my mind, because she quickly went on to admit that it didn't quite settle anything, but pointed out that it wasn't exactly a clear issue since Grant's objections to the girl were more personal than social, and that the main thing was that he and his family see my point of view, and that this was what she was trying to do. So then I weakly sidestepped the whole thing by saying it wasn't really up to me at all, it was up to Lula. So then they both looked at each other and she said of course that was it, and there was nothing I could do but call Lula. She came out, and I had one crumb of satisfaction, that she didn't even try to sit down in the presence of Mrs. Harris, but stood there, first on one foot and then on the other, saying yes ma'am and no ma'am in a frightened way that showed her up for the servant girl she really was.

Mrs. Harris had nothing to say to her of what we had been talking about but merely offered her a job and told her the pay and a few other things about it. But when Lula got it through her head what was meant she at once acted very shifty and confused, and said she would have to think it over before she could give her answer. Mrs. Harris said if there was something she wanted to talk to *me* about privately—she would be very glad to wait. But Lula said it wasn't that. She had the offer of a job somewhere, but she wouldn't know until late this afternoon when she returned from Brooklyn, where she had to go to see about it.

I had heard nothing up to then about any job that she had, but almost before Mrs. Harris had got through saying she would stop by again later in the afternoon Lula was gone. She disappeared, grabbed her hat and streaked out of the apartment without saying a word to me or anybody. Grant, however, acted as though a great load had been lifted from his mind and proposed that all three of us go to lunch, and this we did, walking up to the Plaza. Many people came up and spoke to us, and Mrs. Harris presented them to me in the most respectful way, and yet all the time we were eating I kept having an uneasy feeling that something lurked back of it and that I didn't know what it was.

But I had to find out, if I could, so I suggested to Grant that he take his mother to a matinee, and off they went. I jumped in a cab, came home and called Mr. Hunt at his office. He knew nothing about Mrs. Harris's scheme for Lula but at once warned me there must be something wrong with it. Then he thought for a moment or two and told me that his guess would be that Mrs. Harris would issue invitations to a large party in my honor, knowing all the time that with Lula in the house I would not dare attend. Then I would

94

be put in the position with Grant of refusing to have anything to do with his mother. It dawned on me then the clever trick that Mrs. Harris was trying to play on me. For the result would be, so long as she had Lula in her house, that I would not dare go there and probably Grant wouldn't either, for that matter. Thus, while getting credit in Grant's eyes for doing something very gracious about Lula, she would be driving a wedge between me and Grant that could only sink deeper all the time.

I knew then that I had to do something about Lula, but I still didn't want to put myself in the position of backing down on my point. If I could make it appear that Lula had got a job herself, and in that way I got rid of her, at any rate I had stood by my guns, and while Grant had also stood by his, he and the whole family had found out I was not to be trifled with.

Chapter Ten

As soon as Mr. Hunt hung up I called Mr. Holden. He was at his hotel, fortunately, and almost before I had time to take the cocktail tray out of the living room and put some fresh ice and glasses on it he was announced and then I let him in and he was walking around looking at everything in a very interested way and making comments on everything he saw. He seemed to know a great deal about American history and when he picked up one of the Aztec knives, told me I should read Prescott's "Conquest of Mexico" and I would "find out how quick the ruling class can tear a man's heart out," as he put it. Some other time I would have been pleased to hear intelligent remarks about Grant's work, but just then I didn't care how the ruling classes tore out hearts. I told him about Lula, and when I got to the things in the bathroom he laughed loudly and didn't wait to hear any more. "So you want somebody to take her off your hands?"

"Dead or alive."

"That's easy. Where's your telephone?"

"What are you going to do?"

"Put in a call."

I took him in the bedroom and stood there while he picked up the receiver, but he cocked his head on one side in a way that meant get out, so there was nothing for me to do but leave him there and close the door. I could hear him talking some little time, and started to make him a brandy and soda. Then I remembered he didn't drink, and I had a cup of coffee waiting for him by the time he was through. He came back in the living room, sat down beside the coffee, thanked me for it and laughed. "It's all arranged."

"What did you do?"

"Found her a job."

"Where?"

"Karb's."

"But they're on strike. There's no job for her there."

"Oh, yes, there is. Strike-breaker."

He said this as though it were an amusing piece of news, but I was greatly startled by it. "Do you mean to say that you, a union organizer, actually proposed that Karb's take on a strike-breaker?"

"They've already taken on fifty—or so I heard. I haven't been in close touch with the thing lately. One more won't hurt."

"But it's—asking a favor of the enemy."

"In all warfare there's an occasional exchange of prisoners. It makes things simple."

"I don't believe you're unfriendly with Karb's at all."

"I? Unfriendly with Karb's? I should say not. Carrie, the wars are fought on the field. The treaties are signed on a table. But a table discussion should be carried on by gentlemen who understand each other. I always observe the courtesies of the field for the sake of the discussion at the table. Asking a harmless little favor with a wink in my eye—"

"They didn't see the wink."

"They felt it. It traveled over the wires by a rare form of television."

"In other words, you're a Welshman."

"I am not. I am a naturalized American, 100%."

He took a little American flag out of his pocket, made out of silk and attached to a pin, and stuck it in his lapel, and it was all so silly I couldn't help but laugh. We sat and drank coffee and he talked about the labor movement and then Lula came in and he certainly made quick work of her. She didn't want to take the job at first, said her Brooklyn opening would materialize in a week and until it did she wanted to stay with me. He brushed this aside at once and then she said she wouldn't be a strike-breaker at Karb's because this would make her a scab. He said in reality she wouldn't be a strike-breaker at all but a union spy, "particularly noble and above reproach," as he put it, and then he turned very hard and stern and in almost no time he made her pack and bundled her out of there so fast I hardly had time to slip her the ten dollars I had decided to give her. We were still laughing about how simple it had been when the door opened, and Grant came in with his mother.

■　　　■　　　■

They stood there looking at us and for a moment I didn't know what to do and didn't much care what I did, to tell the truth, as I was so happy over the great load that had been lifted from my mind, but Mr. Holden took charge in a most impressive way. He bowed as though he were in some royal palace, and without waiting for me to introduce me he recalled himself to Grant and there was nothing for Grant to do but introduce Mr. Holden to his mother, which he did very coldly. On their side it was all very stiff and snooty but this didn't faze Mr. Holden a bit. He laughed and said: "We're celebrating a deliverance."

"Oh?"

Grant tried to sound casual but the quick way he turned his head showed he was quite curious.

"Yes, the lovely Lula has had an offer of employment, has accepted it, and taken her sad farewell. Not that it didn't break her heart. But she went."

Mrs. Harris sat down at this piece of news, stared at Mr. Holden and seemed to turn into a block of ice. But Grant, as it finally got through his head, started to laugh and said: "So. She took it. And I thought that Brooklyn job was a phony."

"Oh, it wasn't the Brooklyn job. My, my, the lady had all sorts of offers, didn't she? All tributes to her sterling character, no doubt. No, this was still another job. I had the honor of being bearer of the happy tidings and now, having discharged my historic function, as Trotsky would have put it, I'll be on my way."

He got up, but Grant still stood between him and the door and didn't move. They were facing each other for a moment, and then Grant laughed again. "Holden, I think you're a liar."

"Others have thought so but I've survived it."

"I think Carrie called you up and asked you to get that nuisance out of here so she could sidestep all these imaginary issues she's been raising. Right?"

"Since I'm already called a liar my testimony on that point would be worthless."

"Anyway, thanks—and let's have a drink."

"More coffee would be fine."

I felt so happy I almost forgot it was I who had to make the coffee, since what I had already served was cold by now, and then when I did go out in the kitchen I couldn't remember where anything was and it all took me a long time. But when I finally did get back with the coffee, and an old-fashioned with Scotch for Mrs. Harris and rye and seltzer for Grant, things were very unpleasant in there. Mrs. Harris's voice sounded shrill, as it had that afternoon at the cocktail party, and she was telling Grant that since she had gone to all this trouble to give the girl work she thought the least that was due her was that she be consulted before anything was done about Lula. Grant told her she was forgetting that the only person who had any real say in the matter was Lula and that it was a free country and that Lula had done what she wanted to do. I said nothing, but served the things I had brought, and was so glad I had turned the tables on her that I didn't trust myself to say anything at all. Grant was happy too, although of course he never for a moment penetrated what his mother was up to, and wanted to smooth things down. He raised his glass to Mr. Holden, who raised his coffee cup. Then he raised his glass to me and I raised my coffee cup, but when he raised his glass to Mrs. Harris she made no move toward her old-fashioned but went right on with her tirade. Then Grant, Mr. Holden and myself sipped in silence while she talked, getting louder all the time, and then Grant got impatient with her and began to talk back, saying it was his home, not hers, and I sat back and wondered whether I could purr if I tried.

During all of this Mr. Holden said not a word but coldly studied her. She had got up by now and was yelling down at Grant, where he still sat taking quick gulps out of his highball and nervously drawing at a cigarette. Mr. Holden got up, went over to where they were and put his arms around her. She jerked around, raised her face to his, and her eyes were simply horrible to see. But he smiled down at her, laid his fingers on her cheek and patted it. "Now why get excited? They're two misguided youngsters, wholly incapable of dealing with the simplest problem, but we don't care, do we?"

"Oh, don't *we?*"

"No—let's leave them to stew in their own juice, which is really what they want to do, for some reason beyond my comprehension. Let's go and have dinner, you and me. I'll forsake my principles and drink a bottle of wine with you, a pale white wine which will pick up the color of your hair...Yes?"

Her eyes grew large and soft, and her whole face took on a dreamy, yielding look. She didn't answer him at once, but looked away from him as though he were seeing stars somewhere in the distance, then took his hand in hers and spoke in a whisper: "I just love the pale white wines."

They barely took time to say their goodbyes, and then they were gone. I suppose he was doing it all for me, and yet I couldn't escape a little twinge of jealousy, or whatever it was, as I watched them go down in the elevator, she looking up at him, he still smiling down at her, for I had probably come to regard him as my property, even if I was married, and I somehow hated the idea of her taking him away from me. But when I went back to the living room I forgot all about that. Grant was still sitting there, a horrible look on his face. For the first time in my life I knew I was looking into the eyes of a killer. I suddenly remembered what Mr. Hunt had told me about Grant's jealousy, and realized why Mrs. Harris had gone out with Mr. Holden and who that look of death was meant for. I was face to face with the real spectre that haunted my marriage.

I prefer not to tell the details of the scene that followed, of what he said, which sounded like the ravings of a lunatic, or of his threats to strangle his mother and Mr. Holden to death. It was frightful and lasted until a late hour. I tried to get him to go out with me for dinner but he wouldn't even hear me, and so I fixed something with what was in the icebox and got him to eat a little of it. But when he quieted down it was even worse, for he seemed to have decided on something, I didn't know what. About eleven o'clock he flung out of the apartment and I at once telephoned Mr. Hunt, to warn him that there might be trouble. Mr. Hunt thanked me and hung up very quickly, and then it was my turn almost to go insane from worrying about what was going to happen. About half past twelve I got a call from Mr. Hunt saying that Grant had been to his mother's house and that there had been a terrible fight, but fortunately Mr. Holden had already gone home after bringing her back from dinner and that, for the moment at least, there would be no violence. Some time after that Grant came home and I managed to get him to bed, but once more there came an outbreak of those sobs which had aroused in me such a peculiar mixture of contempt and pity.

For the next two or three days he hardly seemed to know I was around, and then took to leaving the apartment, as he did while Lula was there. To make it worse, Mr. Holden did not stop at taking Mrs. Harris to dinner once but kept on going around with her. But a columnist got hold of it, for of course a society woman going around with a labor leader was news, and if Grant had been insane before, he turned into a gibbering idiot now. Through a phone call that came in for him one day, when I heard a secretary at the other end say something while I was holding the line, I discovered that he had employed private detectives to trail his mother, and then I knew I had to act.

I called Mr. Holden, got him at his hotel, and pleaded with him not to see Mrs. Harris any more. He listened and laughed. "This is what I've been waiting for, Carrie. It makes my heart sing. So it *does* matter to you, when I start trotting around with another woman?"

"It's not that at all. I—I didn't mean to tell you this. I don't *want* to tell you, and I'm only doing it so you'll understand why I called. It's not on my account. It's on account of my husband."

"What has your husband got to do with it?"

"He—he's jealous of his mother."

I could feel my face getting hot at the cackle of laughter he let out at the other end of the phone, and only half heard what he said about Grant's being a mama's boy, and other things of that kind. But then I cut in on him: "Please don't talk like that any more. This is serious. He—he might kill you. He might kill her. He might kill you both. He's set detectives on your trail already and I'm terrified. Haven't you any regard for your life?"

"It'll be nothing new for me to be shot at. In my business I meet many a fine buck who wants to kill me, and some of them have even hired private thugs to do it. But I'm still here, and I haven't stopped a bullet yet."

"You will if you keep this up."

"I'll drop Mrs. Harris like a hot cake—on one condition."

"Name it. It's granted."

"That you put an end to that silly marriage and come with me to the Coast. I've been ordered West, and I have real work to do. We'll take the plane tonight, do whatever has to be done about your divorce, and that will be the end of Mrs. Harris the Younger and Mrs. Harris the Elder. She's not so elderly, by the way. She's still quite romantic."

"...I can't grant that condition."

"Did you hear what I said? She's not at all elderly."

"Yes, I heard what you said."

I must have sounded very miserable, for his tone changed, and he said: "Carrie, why aren't you honest with me? You don't like it when I tell you she's romantic, and that's the real reason you called me."

"No, it's not at all—"

"*It is!* Are you trying to tell me that I mean less to you than that whippersnapper you're married to? You've trifled with me—and with *him*—long enough. Come back to one of your kind—"

101

"I'm sorry. I can't."

In spite of the harsh words he used he had spoken as though I belonged to him, and I knew I was cutting him to the quick when I still turned him down. There was a long silence at the other end of the line and when he spoke his voice was muffled and strange. "Then it's 'no'?"

"I'm afraid it is."

"Then— his voice was clear and hard this time—"I'm afraid it's 'no' with me too, Carrie. I have my pride too, and the lady likes me."

■　　■　　■

Some time during all this Lula began visiting me in the afternoons after she got off, to sympathize with me over the way I was being treated and to give me news of the strike, which it appeared, was about to be settled. I didn't want to see her, I didn't want to see anybody, and yet I had reached such a state that I dreaded being alone, for all I could find to do with myself was sit and read the books on finance which Grant had accumulated in connection with his position at Harris, Hunt and Harris. I dipped into the Indian books too, but found finance more interesting, and was surprised to see how much of it I could understand, especially when I began to follow daily the financial pages of the New York *Times*. Money in all its phases, as I have mentioned before, is continually fascinating to me.

However, although this helped pass the time, I was lonely and nervous and when Lula showed up I would sit with her just for the sake of company. I always brought her into the kitchen so if Grant came home unexpectedly I could get her out and he wouldn't know she had been there. But he was always very late, so she would usually stay until nine or ten o'clock, of course eat her dinner with me, which I would have to prepare, and leave before he came.

■　　■　　■

One night we talked and talked and talked, and I could hear my mouth say feverish, excited things that seemed to have no meaning and then say them all over again, for I didn't have my mind on what we were talking about at all. Then I realized that Lula didn't either, and that she was eyeing me in a very strange way. Then I looked at my watch and it was half-past one, and I realized why I had been behaving as I had. Down deep inside of me I knew that Grant wasn't coming home, and that was what I had been fighting off.

Lula caught my wrist and looked at my watch too, and came out with her usual remark, which was: "Well, for crying out loud."

"I think I'm a little fast."

"You ain't fast. It's late, Carrie. It's that late I'm almost afraid to go home, but I didn't want to leave you here, all alone in this place—well, ain't he the louse! I declare, it's a shame, the way he treats you—"

"He's no louse, and how he treats me is my own affair. He had business—in Newark. He—"

"Newark? He told you that? He—"

"He's had to take a late train!"

"Train, my eye! Don't you get it, Carrie? He's walked out on you. It's the old powder he's taken. He's not coming home—"

I almost threw her out. When I had myself under some kind of control I went in the living room and sat by the window and waited. I saw the milk-wagon horse come up Second Avenue, saw the sun come up over the river, saw the people hurrying over toward the Lexington Avenue subway to go to work. He didn't come.

Around nine o'clock I went in and bathed and changed my clothes. I was making myself some coffee when I heard the papers delivered outside. I hate things lying in an apartment hallway, so I went out and got them. Once more my picture was all over the front page of the tabloid that had been running the story of my life, and there was the headline:

"HARRIS DESERTS CINDY"

I knew then who had been giving them all their information about my girlhood, my life with Grant and all the rest of it, why Lula had stayed with us, why she kept coming back, even after she had been put out. I put on my hat and coat, went downstairs, had the doorman get me a cab and went over to the address she had given me. It was a rooming house. To save herself the climb of announcing me the woman gave me the room number and told me to go on up. And there, sure enough, was Lula, lying on a sofa in a negligee, smoking. A newspaper man whom I remembered from Mrs. Hunt's cocktail party was sitting in a chair writing in a notebook. Another was at a typewriter that had been placed in one corner of the room.

I went over to Lula and without waiting for her to say, "Well, for crying out loud," I slapped her face. She jumped up, her eyes blazing, and I slapped her again, and that time I knocked her down. I went over to the typewriter, pulled out the sheet that was in the machine, scooped up all the other sheets I could see and tore them up. I went over to the man with the notebook, and he backed into a corner and tried to shove it into his pocket. I picked up a chair, drove straight at his head with it and he went down. I grabbed the notebook and tore that up. It must have taken me a minute to tear all the pages into little pieces, but I made a thorough job of it and all during that time the three of them, two on the floor and one behind the typewriter, merely blinked at me. Not a word was spoken.

On the floor Lula's cigarette was beginning to burn a hole in the carpet. I went over, stepped on it, turned on my heel and walked out.

Chapter Eleven

I got into another cab, went down to Mr. Holden's hotel and walked up to the desk. "Mrs. Harris calling on Mr. Holden."

"Yes, Mrs. Harris. Mr. Holden left word you were to come right up."

I was so wrought up from loss of sleep and what had happened with Lula that I was in the elevator before it occurred to me how surprising that was, that he was expecting me and had left word for me to come up. Then it occurred to me that it might be the other Mrs. Harris, Grant's mother, that he was expecting, and I had a panicky impulse to have the elevator take me down again and run away without seeing him at all. However, it was me he was expecting, for I was no sooner in his apartment before he put his arms around me and drew me very close, and he was so sincere about it that it was impossible to resent it. Indeed, I didn't want to resent it, for it felt so good to be loved, regardless of what I was, that I put my arms around him too, and when he kissed me I kissed back, and held him close and felt very deeply moved. So, when he told me how he had called me up as soon as he read the paper, and had then been waiting for me to come, it was all the harder for me to state my business, for it wasn't what he thought it was at all.

I took from my handbag the bank book showing the deposit I had made as treasurer of the union, as well as the small account book which gave the names of the members, and all other records insofar as I had anything to do with them. I then made out a check payable to him covering the whole amount and laid it all down in front of him. "There. I think you'll find that everything balances, and you can endorse the check over to whoever is elected to take over my duties."

"Well, well, well. I never saw such a grim face in my life or such neat columns of figures. What is this, Carrie?"

"I'm quitting as treasurer of the union."

"Tut, tut."

"I can't go on with it."

"I wasn't asking you to go on with it, and I've little interest today in the treasurer of the union. It's a sweet red-haired girl I have my mind on, but—let's get it over with. What's come up between you and the union? They settled the strike, by the way."

"Nothing's come up between me and the union, but I think I'm going into business and I have to square up all accounts.

"You've walked out on Grant, Lula and the union. All right, besides business, now what?"

"...I don't know."

"I do. You take off your hat and stay here."

He was so simple and honest, and it seemed so fine, after all the turmoil and mean schemes I had faced, that I ached

105

to take off my hat, as he said, and let him take charge of me from then on. But I knew the pain inside of me wouldn't stop if I did. Yet now I knew he was a part of my life, something he had not really been before, and that I had to be honest with him. I got up, put my arms around him, pulled his head down and kissed him. "I want to say something."

"I'm listening to you, Carrie."

"I think you're swell."

"Go on."

"I think you mean more to me than I ever realized you did. I think in a little while I'll be able to think about you in the way you want me to, and then perhaps I'll mean still more to you."

"If that's possible."

"It's possible...But now—I've got to face this thing out. You're wrong if you think I married Grant for money, position or anything else except the one reason you would respect. I—loved him—and you have to let me get through this in my own way."

"Then I'm not to see you?"

"I *want* to see you. You'll have to let me see you—because I haven't anybody else. But—oh, I'm all mixed up."

"We'll talk about the weather, is that it?"

"Yes. And I'm afraid we'll talk about Grant too, and I'll be a terrible nuisance, and—"

"I've a fine idea. We won't talk at all. Would you like that?"

I pulled him to me again and we stood there for a few minutes, very close, not talking at all.

■   ■   ■

There was no taxi when I went out on the street so I started to walk, but I had a sensation in my legs as though I were made of air and would go floating off some place. In spite of what I had said to him at the end it was Lula and the union I kept thinking about, and I knew I had cut every tie that bound me to the world I had left.

■   ■   ■

106

When I came in sight of the apartment house I began to walk faster, then I made myself slow down and fought off the hope I could not help feeling within me. Yet my heart almost stopped beating when I entered the apartment and heard somebody moving about in the bedroom. I paused a moment and pulled myself together, especially so there would be no smile on my face or anything, for I did not want to appear too eager. Then, as casually as I could, I went in there.

Steamer trunks, shirts and suits of clothes were piled all over the bed and a strange woman, in a maid's uniform, was standing at the chest of drawers, taking everything out. When she saw me she stopped what she was doing and looked very frightened. It was a moment or two before I could speak. "What are you doing here?"

"We come for Mr. Harris's things."

She spoke with a German accent and I was slow in understanding her, but the "we" caught my ear. "What do you mean 'we'? Who else is here with you?"

"Mrs. Harris, Miss."

"Where?"

"I don't know, Miss. She come. She is here."

I went in the living room and she was already coming toward me, her arms outstretched. "My dear! I called you. I called you three times. But then the dear boy had to have something to wear and I—"

"You borrowed his key and sneaked in when you knew I wasn't here. Because of course you called—three times."

When I said that she somehow changed her mind about putting her arms around me but she kept the smile on her face, turned to a chair and started to sit down, at the same time taking charge of me in a very patronizing way. "Sit down, Carrie. I can see we have things to tell each other."

I picked up the chair from behind her and pushed it back against the wall so she almost fell down, so at any rate the grand manner had a crimp put in it. "I do the inviting around here. Suppose we stand up."

"Very well, my dear."

"So you've finally taken Grant away from me?"

"Not I—oh, not I. I don't think he told you, he's so kind he couldn't hurt anybody—but he still loves Muriel, Carrie."

"He never loved Muriel."

"Ah, if you only knew—"

"I know all I want to know or need to know. After a month of insulting me, of scheming against me, of torturing Grant in every way that you know, you've finally succeeded in making two people unhappy and breaking up their marriage, in doing everything you started out to do. You've come here for his clothes and personal effects, and all I have to say to you is, take them and get out."

I stepped very close to her as I said that and I trembled with a desire to slap her face. If I hadn't already slapped Lula's face I would have done it, but somehow I couldn't just go around slapping faces. She started to say something, then didn't, and stood there with the smile still hanging on her face, but it was beginning to be weak and frightened. I pointed to the bedroom. "Get in there with your maid. Make it as quick as you can and when you're ready to go you may give me the key that you let yourself in with. I'll not let you leave here until I have it."

"Yes—certainly."

■   ■   ■

She called the elevator boys to help her take the trunks down and when she had gone it was my turn to storm around there and act like a lunatic all by myself. I broke out into a perfect hysteria of rage and kept weeping and moaning because I hadn't slapped her face. If I had I think my whole future life would have been different, because it would have satisfied me and from then on I would have had no impulse to do anything against her. But I hadn't slapped her face, and all I could feel was a rising surge of fury against her. She was the only person in my life I had ever hated, and from then I could feel nothing but an obsession to get back at her.

■   ■   ■

Around three or four o'clock came the reaction. I began to cry and lay down on the sofa, trying to stop. When I did I remembered that I not only hadn't had any sleep but I hadn't had anything to eat either. I went in and bathed my eyes, then went out. At some lunch room down on Second Avenue

I had a sandwich and a glass of milk. When I came out on the street again I remember standing there looking around, trying to decide which was uptown and which was downtown. I have no recollection of going back to the apartment or of what I did when I got there. The next thing I knew it was night and I was lying on the bed, still dressed and feeling as though I had been in some kind of stupor. But what woke me was that I was cold. I got up, took off my clothes, and put on my pajamas and went back to bed again, under the covers this time. Grant flitted through my mind but I didn't cry or feel badly that he wasn't there. I seemed incapable of feeling *anything*, and next thing I knew it was morning.

After a night's rest, however, I was capable of feeling, for a quick stab of pain shot through me when I realized I was alone. I got up at once, so I could be doing something in order not to think. I took a bath, slipped into a suit of house pajamas I had bought, and made myself breakfast. I had cereal, milk, coffee, toast and an omelet, taking time to beat the omelet thoroughly so it tasted good and I could eat every bit of it. When I was through I washed everything up clean and put it back exactly where it had been when I came there. I dressed carefully, went out and walked over to Bloomingdale's, where I bought a traveling bag which I brought back with me in a taxi. It was what they call airplane luggage, almost as big as a trunk, but it was made out of nice leather and had hangers in it, which I especially wanted for the new things I had bought after I got married. I had the elevator boy bring it up for me and as soon as I was in the apartment with it I changed into the house pajamas again and packed. I was careful to put in everything that was mine and to take nothing that wasn't mine. When I had finished I put the house pajamas on top and changed into the green dress I had bought before I met Grant, for I didn't want to wear anything associated with my marriage. I closed the new bag and also the one I had brought when I came.

That night I called Mr. Holden. I met him for dinner, then brought him to the apartment and we talked. He accepted what I had told him and made no personal advances at all. He spoke at length about his plans for organizing workers in the West and said it would be imperative for him to leave for the Coast within two weeks. I tried to imagine myself going with him, tried to believe I would be lonely after he left. I couldn't think of anything but Grant and the bitterness I felt against the woman who had taken him away from me.

■　　　■　　　■

Next day I went down into the financial district to look around with a view to starting a business for myself. From what I knew of the eating habits of people in Wall Street, as the result of my work at Karb's, I felt there would be an opportunity for a place run like a little club, where men could come in, see their friends, be served quickly and get back to their offices without consuming too much time. As a matter of fact, there are a number of luncheon clubs on lower Broadway, but most of them are both expensive and exclusive. What I had in mind was a place to be located right in one of the big office buildings so that the customers could eat without even leaving the building. But of course it was all tied up with the question of rent and the kind of bargain I could make.

I saw the superintendents of several large buildings and while most of them were full up, one place had a space and they were willing to make concessions, so that things looked very favorable. The next two or three days I put in talking to the restaurant supply houses and they were very attentive to me and willing to extend credit, so that even with my limited capital it looked as though I would be able to make a start. And yet I didn't seem able to make up my mind about anything and would come home every night and sit there and look at my packed luggage and think about Grant. Then Mr. Holden would call and we would go to dinner, and then I would come home again and go to bed and it would be all gray and depressing and I didn't seem to take any interest in whether I could start a business or not.

■　　　■　　　■

One day I came home earlier than usual and found a note from Mr. Hunt saying he had called and giving his number, with the request that I call him. My heart began beating fast, and I called.

"Carrie, I've got to see you."

"What about?"

"Money."

It was a disappointment, but after a moment I said: "I'm amply provided for, thank you."

"I said I had to see you and all I want to know is, are you home or aren't you?"

"...Yes."

"I'm coming down."

So in a half hour he was there. Before he arrived I phoned the desk that he was to be sent up and then I hurriedly got out Scotch and a seltzer siphon and opened the Scotch. He took the drink I made for him, crossed his legs and remarked: "God, but Granny's a fool."

"I thought we had agreed that Grant was the victim of something he couldn't very well help."

"I hate victims of things they can't very well help. I hate victims. Even a Chinese war victim has a very stupid look, to my eyes. Did you ever notice those people? They don't really look bright."

"So?"

"Granny's a victim. To hell with them all."

"The Chinese children don't look so stupid. They look sweet."

"Granny's no child."

"He is to me."

"To me he's a fool—just a plain fatheaded sap. And if you take that to mean that I think you're all right—O.K., that's what I do think. However, that's not what I came here for."

I waited and he kept rubbing the moisture on his glass with his thumb, which seemed to be a habit of his, and then he said: "I've been selected to buy you off."

"...I don't know what you mean."

"I mean, find out how much you'll take to get a divorce and forget the whole unfortunate incident. I believe they stipulate a trip to Reno, so the thing can be washed up quickly and quietly."

"...Well. I had thought of you as a friend."

"That's exactly the way I think of myself."

"This doesn't sound much like it."

"No, it doesn't. I'm surprised how unpleasant it sounds. It has a regular Judas ring to it. Nevertheless, it's supposed to be friendly—on my part, at least. But I'm only the fiscal agent."

"If you don't mind, I don't want to hear any more."

"Carrie."

"Yes, Mr. Hunt?"

"Suppose you call me Bernie."

"All right, Bernie, but I warn you if I hear any more about this I'm liable to pick up an ice cube and hit you in the eye with it. I've taken quite a few things in the last few days and this could be the straw that broke the camel's back. Why did you come up here with any such proposal as this? If you think I'm 'all right' does that mean I could be bought off just like some floosie?"

He came over and half knelt beside me and touched my hand. "Now we're getting somewhere. Now comes the friendly part. What did I tell you the last time we talked about this?"

"You mean at your home that day?"

"Yes."

"...You told me I was sunk."

He was so straightforward there was no use pretending I didn't remember. He must have seen that it upset me, for he waited a moment before he went on. Then he said, very quietly: "That's right. That's what I told you. Carrie, you're still sunk. It's all over. Now it's simply a question of how much."

"It's simply a question of me being sick of the whole miserable mess, and I don't want to hear any more about it."

"Let's go into that. Why not?"

"That woman, for one thing."

"Go on."

"Do you think I'd give *her* the satisfaction of thinking she could—*buy me off?*"

"Listen: When I take money off a louse I figure she's still a louse but I've got the money."

I couldn't help laughing at this and he laughed too. "And believe me, when I say louse I don't mean butterfly. I've been

112

her son-in-law for five years and I never saw anything like her. But never mind that, let's get back to you. There's twenty-five thousand bucks in it for you if you'll get on the train for Reno in some kind of reasonable time and my advice is: take it."

"I can't."

"All right then, here comes the real Judas part, only I'm selling *them* out this time, not you. Things haven't been going as well with them as perhaps you think. You've heard of Uncle George, haven't you?"

"Yes."

"Uncle George is the senior partner in the brokerage house of Harris, Hunt and Harris. I keep him out of the brokerage business pretty well, so that part's all right. But I can't keep him out of the Harris estate. He manages that, and he made mistakes. Do you want the details?"

"No."

"They were pretty serious. George got clever, just after we got in the war and for a while it was fine, but then afterwards the Harris millions began to melt. That might be the reason Grant can't get the money he wants to dig up those Central American Indians. And it might be the reason that George was so enthusiastic when Mama decided that Grant ought to marry Muriel. That's all conjecture. I'm not admitted to the inner councils of the Harris estate, but this much I know: things aren't so good. Twenty-five thousand dollars, if you take it now, is a good offer. It's about all they can pay. If you wait too long the offer may be withdrawn. They may not be in a position to pay *anything*...Carrie, *take it*."

"I told you—I can't do it."

Chapter Twelve

The next day I dressed to go out and resume preparations for starting a business. But somehow, after I got my hat on, I didn't want to go out. I kept sitting there and all I could think of was: $25,000, $25,000, $25,000. It kept drumming through my head and I tried to get my mind off it but couldn't. I kept telling myself that at a time like this, when all that I really wanted was to come out of it with a clear conscience, I shouldn't let my interest in money cause me to do something which later I would be ashamed of. But I kept thinking about it and not only that, I kept calculating all the things I could do with it, for of course, with that much capital, I could start a business at once, and a much bigger business than I had had in mind when I had started my inquiries a few days before. And then I thought: Well, why *not* take it? Next thing I knew I had taken off my hat and was sitting there in the bedroom at the head of the bed looking at the telephone. Under it, with one corner sticking out, was Mr. Hunt's note with his number on it. I lifted the telephone. Then I clapped my hand on the contact bar at once. For it shot through my mind: If I call him, then it's going to be $25,000. If I don't call him, then he may call me.

I put on my hat again and went gaily out. I felt better than I had in a month. I walked down to the St. Regis, went into the King Cole Room and had a martini cocktail. Then I went into the dining room and had a fine lunch. It cost three dollars without the tip, and it was worth it. I walked over to the Music Hall, saw a picture. When I got back to the apartment there was a wire notice and when I called it was from Mr. Hunt asking me to call him. This made me feel in the humor for a nice dinner, with pleasant talk about grand opera, and literature and the capitals of Europe. I called Mr. Holden.

∎   ∎   ∎

Next morning I was awakened by the phone ringing. I was afraid to answer for fear it would be Mr. Hunt and that they put him through without finding out whether I wanted to talk. So I just let it ring. Then I bathed and dressed quickly and made myself some breakfast. Two or three times the phone rang and I didn't answer, but I thought it advisable to stay in. It was a long wait, but shortly after lunch there came the ring on the buzzer and when I opened the door he was there. I had rubbed all the rouge off my face so I looked very white, and acted very sad. Also, I acted quite absent-minded, and waited at least five minutes before remembering to fix him a drink. He began practically where he had left off, telling me to take the money, that I would have to get a divorce eventually and that I was a fool to let this opportunity slip by to cash in on it for whatever I could. I listened in a very melancholy way, and then, as he got well warmed up, I buried my head in a sofa pillow and began to weep, at any rate as well as I could, though I was afraid to let him see my face for fear there wouldn't be any tears in my eyes. But when I could feel them running down my cheeks I straightened up and let him put his arms around me and pat me and wipe them away with his handkerchief. Then I began to talk in a very desperate way about the six sleeping tablets I took last night so I didn't wake up until one o'clock this afternoon and how I was going to take more and how if they didn't work I was going to throw myself from the window, and then I wept very loud and said: "After all she's done to me—and she thinks—she can—get rid of me—for twenty-five thousand bucks."

He made no reply to this but I could feel him sitting there beside me on the sofa and he was silent so long I decided to peep and see what was the matter with him. He was looking at me with one eye shut and the other eye open, in so comical a way that I had to burst out crying again to keep from laughing. He got up, stood in front of me for a moment, then kicked my foot. "Carrie, every time I see you I like you better...I'll borrow your bath for a moment."

He disappeared, then came back. "Funny thing. I couldn't find any sleeping tablets in that cabinet."

"I feel just terrible."

"In other words, they've got to up it?"

In reply to this I merely moaned, "Twenty-five thousand bucks!"

He drained his highball, picked up his hat, said, "I'll see what I can do," and walked out. I neglected to fasten the door after him, so it was most unfortunate when he popped back in again, to get his stick, and found me doing cartwheels in the middle of the floor. He came over to me, gave me a little kiss on one cheek, winked, and left.

■   ■   ■

Next day he was back, and I wept and bawled a great deal louder, and I let him take a bottle of sleeping tablets away from me just as I was about to swallow them all. He argued with me a great deal, but came up to $30,000. But I still held out.

■   ■   ■

The next day I had a very bright idea, which was to sue Mrs. Harris for $1,000,000 charging alienation of Grant's affections. I thought if I got a lawyer and actually did this it might be a pretty good weapon against her and that if she settled I could withdraw the suit afterwards. But that would mean more newspaper publicity, for which I felt nothing but horror. So when Mr. Hunt came I contented myself with talking about it. I howled that I had changed my mind about killing myself, that I only wanted justice and that I was going to air the whole thing in court and tell all about her designs on Muriel, as well as everything else I knew about her. And in addition to that, I was going to sell the signed story of my life to the newspapers which had made me offers. He argued with me just as solemnly as he had before, but the next day when he came back he was up to $40,000. It went on for two or three days after that and he roared at me just as though he was my bitter enemy, and I roared back in the same way, and all this I am sure was so he could go back to Mrs. Harris with a full account of what had been said. But when he got up to $50,000, and we were roaring louder than we ever had before, he suddenly put his arms around me, lifted the hair from over my ear with one finger and whispered, "Take it."

"Is it the most I can get?"

"If you get a lawyer you can blackjack a bigger settlement. But how much she pays and when she pays it and how much the lawyer takes, I wouldn't like to say. And remember, the lawyer gets his first. This is cash, and it's all yours—$50,000 clear of your expenses to Reno, court costs, and whatever the lawyers charge for the divorce.

"I'll take it."

So then I made him a drink and I had a little one, and we laughed and he said unquestionably it was the best bargain I could have made, looking at it from what I would get out of it. From what he had let drop about the family finances I thought it was too, and anyway, I had said yes, so there was no use wondering any more.

■　　　■　　　■

It astonished me how quickly it was all arranged once the main bargain had been made. I met Mr. Hunt in a lawyer's office in the RKO Building and we went all over it. I was to get $25,000 cash, have all my expenses paid to Reno and back, as well as my hotel bill while I was there, and all costs of the divorce suit which I was to bring against Grant on the ground of desertion or whatever the lawyers in Reno should advise. Another $25,000 was to be placed in trust for me with the lawyers in Reno, and paid me as soon as the divorce was granted. Two or three days later I went there again to sign papers and as soon as this was over Mr. Hunt picked up Mrs. Harris's check for $25,000 and handed it to me. It startled me to see her handwriting on the check, very small and neat, and to learn that her first name was Agnes. It seemed too sweet a name for such a viper.

I deposited the check in my checking account, for I hadn't yet decided what I was going to do with the money. When I got home I tried to feel pleased that I was worth over $26,000 now, an amount I would have regarded as a fortune less than a year before, and that I would be worth more than $50,000 in another few weeks. But I couldn't seem to enjoy the realization as much as I had expected to. At first I told myself it was because the silly battle with Mr. Hunt was all over and the excitement had died down. But what I kept thinking about was that neat little "Agnes Harris" at the bottom of that check, and I knew that what I had been afraid of had come to pass: I had done something I wish I hadn't done. Whether I had her $25,000 or not, the victory was hers, not mine, and I hated her all the more.

Two or three days after that Mr. Hunt took me to the plane, driving the car himself. Going over the Williamsburg bridge was when it swept over me that I was cutting all ties with Grant, so by the time the plane went down the field and then came wheeling up to the gate to take me away I was fighting back tears, and they were real ones this time, not the phony ones I had been shedding the last two or three weeks. He must have sensed the state I was in, for he kept talking very rapidly about the fine accommodations I would have aboard the plane, but at the same time giving my hand little quick squeezes. At last I could stand it no longer, and had to ask him what was really on my mind. "Did you— have you any messages for me?"

His face hardened and he sounded quite savage when he spoke. "I told you, Grant's a fool. No, I have no messages. I haven't seen him, as a matter of fact. He's not in town. He's up in the country, recuperating from all he's been through—I hope you get that. From all *he's* been through.

They opened the gate then and I started for the plane. He caught me in his arms, gave me a quick hug and a little kiss. "Listen, I'm a Harvard man too, but it didn't have any effect. Everything I've said to you about how much I think of you still stands. So when you get back I want to see you."

"Me, too."

He took my shoulders and jerked them back, then tilted my face up very high. "Chin up."

■   ■   ■

It seemed amazing to me that we reached Kansas City by ten o'clock that night, for Kansas City had always seemed very far away and not at all a part of my life. And yet I was there. I had watched half the United States slip by under me, had flown over St. Louis, had seen the Mississippi River, like a dark snake twisting through the lights, had set my watch back an hour, and even in New York it was only eleven o'clock. I had a cup of coffee in the airport restaurant, got back on the plane again, fastened my seat belt and in another minute we were off.

I could have had a berth but had asked Mr. Hunt not to take one, as I wanted to look. About one o'clock the moon came up and around two or three o'clock we began flying over the Rocky Mountains. It was early November but even at that season of the year some of the peaks had snow on them, and it looked very white and still down there and terribly wild. Then it began to get light and I could see still better, and I got some idea of how big the United States really is. Then off to the left, and a little behind me, appeared a light in the sky. I thought it was some kind of plane beacon at first and then I thought it was a light on a plane I couldn't see. But finally I realized it was the morning star, and I felt sad and depressed again, for it was behind me.

■　　■　　■

It turned out that a reservation had already been made for me at the Riverside and I went up to look at my apartment. It was a pleasant suite with a bedroom, sitting room and bath. I suppose Mr. Hunt had seen to that, and done whatever had to be done to permit me to keep it the necessary six weeks. When I raised the question of price I found out the bill was to be sent to Hollowell & Hyde, the lawyers I had been referred to, so I never found out what it cost. However, it was very nice and I at once unpacked, hung up my things, had a bath and changed my dress. Then I went down and had breakfast and looked up Mr. Hyde, who was located in an office building nearby. Walking over there I could not but admire the clean, fresh look that Reno had, with mountains in the distance and the Truckee River running through the center of the town within a few steps of the hotel. At least they call it the Truckee River, but it was not a river like the Hudson, or any river I had ever seen. It was nothing but a rapid stream you could throw a stone across, but the water was clear and green and boiled along in a picturesque way.

My talk with Mr. Hyde was very brief. He asked me a few questions, then said the simplest thing would be for me to charge cruelty, and he would go over the details with me when the time came. He warned me not to register at any hotels outside the state during this period when I would be establishing my residence in Nevada. However, he said it would be all right for me to take automobile trips into California, or wherever I wanted, provided I got back to Reno the same night. So within an hour I was back at the hotel with nothing to do but wait.

119

During my negotiations with Mr. Hunt I hadn't said a word to Mr. Holden about what I expected to do, for I was afraid if he found out I was leaving for Reno he would arrange to leave with me, and this I didn't want. I didn't even call him up to say goodbye. So now I sent him a telegram explaining why I had left, then went to bed and got some much-needed sleep. Whether it was the high altitude or the letdown from the strain I had been under I don't know, but I slept most of that day and the next and had my meals sent up from room service. So it seemed surprising that around four o'clock the next afternoon the phone rang and the desk said he was downstairs. I told them to have him wait, then dressed as quickly as I could and had him sent up.

He only had about two hours, as he was going to San Francisco, and he was rather different from what he had been any other time I had seen him. He was usually rather flowery in his talk and had a lot of jokes, but now he had very little to say and it was quite brief and to the point. I was to stay here and get my divorce. Where he would be during that time he didn't know, as it was a waterfront strike he was to take charge of and he would be constantly on the move from Seattle clear down to Los Angeles and possibly even San Diego. But whenever he could he would slip over to see me and now and then we would have an evening together. As soon as I was free we would be married and then leave for wherever his work called. I made no objection to any of this, and yet it all seemed remote and not at all in line with my life.

■   ■   ■

Within two or three days after he had left I discovered that passing six weeks in Reno was going to be very tiresome. I met several people around the hotel, most of them ladies who were also waiting for their divorces. They apparently slept all day and toured the clubs all night and they invited me to come with them, so one night I made the rounds. There were many places in town and I think we went to them all, but they didn't interest me much as I never gamble and I didn't care to go any more. I decided I wanted a car, for there were many places I wanted to see in the vicinity and particularly I wanted to visit Goldfield, on account of the stories Pa Selden had told me about the great days of 1908 when it was booming and he was there. The discovery that I could have a car and still make hardly any impression on my bank account was probably my first realization of how much $25,0000 really was.

After looking around I decided on a small used coupe which I could get for $900. I didn't regard it as an extravagance, for when I left Reno I could resell it for almost what I paid for it, so I would not be out much. It was light blue, with very smart lines, and I thought I looked very well in it. So they gave me driving lessons and by the end of a day I could do everything very confidently, even back. So by the end of two or three days I was ready for my trip to Goldfield.

It was a very long drive, nearly two hundred miles, and I have to confess that a large part of the way I was quite frightened. The road was built over a flat plain covered with gray alkali dust, with only a few tufts of dry grass showing, and this plain extended for miles and miles. Only once in awhile would I meet a car, and except for them and an occasional rabbit that would hop across the road I couldn't see a living thing or any sign of human habitation. It was my first close contact with desert land and it was like rattling madly through space that didn't mean anything.

I had started around eight o'clock in the morning. I gassed and had lunch at a little town about halfway down and arrived at Goldfield around supper time. It didn't look at all as Pa Selden had described it or like the pictures he had shown me. For it was practically a ghost town now, and I discovered that some years ago they had had a fire which wiped out most of it, with the ruins still there. But the hotel was the same, a big brick building five or six stories high, with a completely deserted lobby full of the leather furniture and oil paintings that were fashionable thirty years ago. The proprietor came forward to meet me and I said: "Can you let me have a room?"

"Lady," he said, with a very sad smile, "I can let you have a dozen?"

It was all very sad and yet somehow romantic and affected the way the Welsh music did the first night I met Mr. Holden. At dinner the proprietor stopped by my table to ask if everything was all right, and when he found what I had come for he called several men who were in the bar and they came and took off their hats in a very elegant way and sat down at the table with me. I offered them something to drink, and they accepted with the most comical little speeches. They were all men of advanced middle age and they wore the big hats you see in the West, and looked exactly like the illustrations in Western stories. It turned out they were old-timers who had been in Goldfield during its great days, and one of them said he remembered Pa Selden, but I don't believe he did at all. Because they constantly told tall stories to kid me and make my eyes pop open, and yet with the most perfect manners. But they all believed that some day Goldfield would come back, and I think it was this that made it all seem so romantic and so pathetic.

But next morning two or three of them were on hand to guide me around, and ugly as the old gold workings were, I found them completely fascinating. They showed me everything from the big piles of ore, which had turned green with the passage of years, to a new mine that had recently been opened up where they said $750,000 had been spent on equipment with not an ounce of pay dirt taken out yet. Then they took me to an assay office which was a rough shack on a back street, where a man poked his head out and acted very mysteriously while we waited outside for him to let us in. They explained that assaying is a very secret work. But pretty soon we went inside and the assayer talked to me and I thrilled all over when he showed me what he called a "button," which remained in his crucible after he had made his tests, and I realized I was handling a little lump of pure gold and that this was the first step in the production of money.

Part Four:
A MINK COAT

Chapter Thirteen

I left next morning and beyond Tonopah I noticed
something in the road ahead of me. The desert air was
so clear that things were visible for miles before you actually
got to them, and so I drove some little time before I was
sure it was a man, and some little time after that before
I could see a car beside the road down on the desert floor.
He stood up when I approached and motioned me to stop.
This was something I would have been afraid to do
anywhere near civilization, but out there in the desert
everything seemed different and I felt I had to. He was a
small, nervous-looking man of about fifty and wore gray
flannels, a sports coat and felt hat, all very rough and yet
very good quality. He lifted his hat and seemed very
annoyed. "I'll borrow your shovel, if you don't mind."

"Shovel?"

"They took mine out when they washed the car yesterday
and forgot to put it back, damn them."

"But I have no shovel."

He looked at me then for the first time, and his eye was
very sharp. "You have no shovel? Didn't they tell you about
that?"

"Nobody said anything to me about a shovel."

"Never start across this desert without a shovel, a towline
and a jar of water. All right, if you have no shovel we'll
have to hook on the towline."

I got out then and saw what had happened. He had pulled
out for a passing car and the whole shoulder had given way,
dumping him out on the desert floor, where his wheels were
buried up to the axles in the alkali dust. What he wanted
the shovel for was to dig them out and probably sprinkle
enough gravel in front of them to enable him to get back
on the road. He wasted no time in explanations, however,

but at once got the towline out of his car, made it fast to his front axle and, as soon as I had pulled up a few feet, to my rear axle. Then he got in his car, took the wheel and tole me to pull up until the towline was tight. This I did. When my car stalled I started it again and he yelled: "All right, give her the gun."

I gave her the gun but I didn't move. Then I became aware of a smell of burning rubber, and he yelled at me to stop. I then assumed I had been spinning my wheels without moving him. But when he came, jumped in my car and pushed me from behind the wheel I discovered it had been a little worse than that. The traction of my wheels had caused the road to slide again, and there I was, hanging over the edge and about to go down in the desert any second. Before he jumped into my car he had unfastened the towline from his own front axle, and now shot my car ahead just as the whole road gave way and spilled out onto the desert in another slide. When we were on safe ground he stopped, took out his handkerchief and mopped his brow. "Close shave."

"Yes, it certainly was."

"Wait a minute."

He got out, unfastened the towline from my rear axle, coiled it up and pitched it in the bottom of my car. "Well, you'll have to give me a ride in to Hawthorne—that's the nearest place I can get a tow car."

So I gave him a ride in to Hawthorne, which was about ten miles, but I let him drive, which relieved my nervousness. As soon as he made sure the garage there would pull him out he thanked me and then asked: "Where do you live?"

"I'm staying in Reno."

"At the Riverside?"

"Yes."

"That's where I live. I'll see you there."

■   ■   ■

Next morning while I was eating breakfast he sat down at my table and began to talk without saying good morning or anything. I found out it was his custom to begin in the middle or perhaps where he left off yesterday, without any

126

preliminaries at all, and while it was an unusual way to do, it was completely a part of him. He was in the same rough clothes, and lit a cigarette, then glanced at me sidewise. "I kept trying to place you yesterday—haven't I met you somewhere before? My name is Bolton. Charles Bolton."

"No, I think not."

"Then I've seen you somewhere. What's your name?"

"Carrie Harris."

"Oh—oh yes, of course. The pictures in the papers. What happened, anyway? Did Agnes bust it up?"

"You *know* her?"

"For years."

"...Do you know Grant?"

"She had three or four brats and I think one of them was a boy. I suppose I know him."

"Yes. As you put it, she busted it up."

"I thought she would when I read the first dispatches about it. She's no angel, Agnes isn't. Is she still good-looking?"

"Yes."

"Something unhealthy about her, though. She's not quite—you know what I mean?—normal."

"I found that out."

"Distinctly alarming, I would say."

"You live here?"

"Lung."

"Oh, I'm sorry."

"Nothing to be sorry about. So long as I stay out here where it's dry it doesn't bother me. White, unmarried, Episcopalian. What are you doing today?"

"Why—nothing."

"Let's go to Tahoe."

"I don't know why not."

"It's all closed up there now so it'll be pleasant to tramp around. We'll drop down to Truckee for lunch and then we'll come back. Do you have galoshes?"

"Do I need them?"

"Snow."

"Oh—fine."

"You'd better wear something rough and warm."

So I hurriedly went down and bought myself a rough skirt and sweater, a beret, woolen stockings, a short reefer coat and stout shoes with galoshes, and about half-past ten we started out in his car. We drove to Truckee, which was only a few miles along the main road to the Coast, then drove up a side road for about a half-hour until we came to Lake Tahoe, and there we parked and walked around. It was marvelous, with the water so clear you could see stones on the bottom, even where it was quite deep, and the fir trees and oaks had snow on them so they looked exactly like Christmas cards. But the mountain air made it quite fatiguing, so after an hour or so we got in the car again and drove back to Truckee, where we had lunch at a little roadside stand. I was so hungry I ate two tongue sandwiches and one made with chopped olive and egg, and had two glasses of milk. Then he said: "I've lived in that hotel for ten years now and I'm a little over-familiar with the menu. Let's go over to Sacramento for dinner."

"All right."

So we took the afternoon driving to Sacramento, and it was one of the most beautiful trips I ever took in my life. We crossed the Sierra Nevada, where at Donner summit the road is 8,000 feet up and away down below you is Donner Lake, which looks like a blue mirror reflecting the sky. All around us was snow, and I was almost sorry when we left it behind us and dropped down into the rolling country of California. We went marching in, rough clothes and all, to a little restaurant he was familiar with, and I had a lobster which was different from the kind I had eaten in the East, as it had no claws, only big legs with little nippers on the end. He said it was really a langouste, but I didn't care what it was, the tail was full of white tender meat and went wonderfully with mayonnaise. After that I had a steak.

■   ■   ■

We started back for Reno around nine o'clock, and on the mountain curves not much was being said. But then suddenly with that trick he had of beginning right in the middle, he said: "So you get the divorce—and then what?"

"Well—a man wants to marry me."

128

"And you?"

"I don't know. And I *won't* know until—"

I stopped, for it swept over me again what had been such an obsession with me in New York. He looked at me sharply and I went on, but my voice sounded hard and not at all humorous, as I intended. "...Until I get back at dear Agnes."

"Now tell me what happened."

I didn't want to tell him, but he kept asking little shrewd questions, and then it began coming out of me in short jerks—not all of what happened, at least on Grant's side, but enough to make sense. After I got a lot of it off my chest I sort of ran down, then added: "I wish there were some way I could snub that Agnes. Her face would be as red as—"

"Ah! Now I get it...So you hate her, is that it?"

"Wouldn't you, if she took your husband—"

"That's got nothing to do with it."

"Oh? Just nothing at all?"

"If that was all you'd hate him, not her. But you don't. You're still in love with him."

"Grant means nothing to me. It's all over—"

"I say you're in love with him. Besides, even if she hadn't taken him away from you, you'd hate her just the same, wouldn't you?"

"She's an unadmirable character."

"And she showed you up for—what did you say you were?"

"...A waitress."

"That's what hurt."

"I'm not ashamed of what I was."

"Suppose, just to pass the time and make a little money, you took a job as waitress in one of our Reno restaurants and then suppose Agnes came in and sat down. What would you do?"

"Pour hot soup down her back."

"You would not. You'd go hide."

"...I guess I would."

"I know you would."

He drove for awhile and then he said: "Well—I don't know how you're going to get back at her. So long as you feel this inferiority she has a bulge on you that no bawling

129

out can ever change. That is, unless you really do enter High Society."

"I *hate* High Society. And how, by the way, could I ever enter it?"

"Oh, that wouldn't be hard. You have money. Not much, but enough. The rest of it's simple. You merely prostrate yourself on the ground and knock your head three times in front of the Great God Horse."

"The Great God—what did you say?"

"I said you have to worship horses. Silly horses, of course. Not circus horses, brewery horses, milk wagon horses, horses that do arithmetic, or any other horses that perform a useful function. Hunters, for example. Horses dedicated to chasing the fox, probably the most futile occupation even seen. Jumpers. Ponies. Ladies' driving horses—in an age that travels by automobile. All sorts of horses, provided they're conspicuously and offensively silly. It's all covered in the literature of the subject. Aldous Huxley and Thorstein Veblen go into it thoroughly, but I do believe some of the shrewdest comment on it was written by Robert W. Chambers. The horse is a symbol. He's this century's pinch of incense on the altars of Caesar—and remember, it was not required that you love Caesar, or believe in his gods or like his friends. Incense was enough. So with High Society. Manners, culture, breeding—they don't mean anything. The horse does. Funny, isn't it, to see people spend millions to get in—on yachts, charities, music and champagne—when one $500 hunter would turn the trick? With $50,000 and a mare for the horse shows, Carrie, you're automatically in. Nobody can keep you out."

"I don't want to be in. I want to—"

"Spit in her eye?"

"Yes...I know one thing I can do. I can give her back her $50,000 and—"

"*What?*"

"Yes. That's it! Now I know what's been pent up in me, making me feel miserable and ashamed. I took that woman's money and—"

"Carrie! That won't make her face turn red. It'll only make her laugh!"

"Oh, don't worry! I won't do anything foolish!"

■   ■   ■

We went on a lot of trips after that, to Carson City and Fallon and Death Valley and all around, and we kept having the discussion. He seemed set on the idea that I had to become a social leader and kept calling himself Pygmalion, whatever he meant by that. But I was wholly indifferent to everything but some scheme for using the money I already had in order to get more money quick and pay back Mrs. Harris the money I had taken off her and perhaps in that way forget her. We took our trips mostly in the afternoon, as he wasn't fond of getting up early, so in the mornings I began dropping in at a brokerage house that was located in an office building down the street from the hotel. In my days of sitting around the apartment in New York I had already become somewhat acquainted with financial matters through studying Grant's books. I wanted to learn more, though at the time I had no exact idea of what I was going to do with my knowledge after I got it. But I asked a lot of questions and followed the ticker and the blackboard and kept reading the *Wall Street Journal*, which was on file there, until I began to have a pretty fair idea of how the whole thing worked. All during this time I could feel stirring in me ambitions much more daring than I had ever had before, and knew that my interest in money, even apart from Mrs. Harris, was becoming a most important factor in my life.

Chapter Fourteen

It was more than a month before I saw Mr. Holden, which didn't surprise me, as the papers were full of the waterfront trouble on the Coast and I assumed he had been pretty busy. But one day I went to see the lawyers again and we went over the divorce case and then when I came back to the hotel Mr. Holden was waiting for me. We went up to my suite and again he was very preoccupied, and seemed to have large affairs on his mind. He began at once asking me questions about my divorce, and wanted to know how soon it would be disposed of. I said in two or three weeks.

131

"Good. That'll just work in with my plans. I'll wash this thing up out there, then stop by for you. As soon as your decree is granted we'll be married, and then—" and here he looked very confident and mysterious—"and *then*, Carrie, you'll see something."

I didn't want to discuss marriage, so I quickly seized the chance to switch over to whatever it was he was talking about. "Yes? And what will I see?"

"Never mind. But it's ready. We've got what we've been waiting for."

"Which is?"

"A break on conditions. It's our market, not theirs. The wheels are going round once more and they've got to settle with labor. And if they don't, labor is going to force them. The war is over, and now we strike."

"When?"

"You'll see. Soon."

From then on things began to move fast and it seemed almost no time before my case was set for trial, so of course when he phoned me from Los Angeles one night I had to tell him when it would come up. So sure enough, the night before I was to appear in court he came again, marched into the hotel with his bags and took a room he had wired for. We had dinner in my suite, however, and he was exuberant and greatly excited. "It'll be the biggest thing in the history of the American labor movement, Carrie. No comic opera affair like what you had at Karb's. This is real."

"You talk a lot but don't tell me what it is."

"We're driving at whole industries."

"...What industries?"

He hesitated, then said: "For the moment, we're keeping it secret, but you'll see. Big industries."

"That'll take quite a while, won't it?"

"Not too long, and this time we land on their button. They're wide open. And we've got the punch."

■   ■   ■

I was so excited I began talking about the trips I had taken around Reno, for I didn't trust myself to discuss his plans anymore. Around ten o'clock I remarked that I had a trying day ahead of me and that I ought to get some sleep. So he went, and I took good care that time to lock the door. Then I went into the bedroom, picked up the telephone and gave the operator Mr. Hunt's home number in New York. I didn't make it person-to-person, as that would be quite expensive, and as it was one o'clock in New York I was pretty sure he would be home. So when the call was put through it was Mrs. Hunt who answered, and I told her who I was and she was very polite but I could tell she was worried. He came to the phone, and as soon as I had answered his inquiries about the divorce, I got down to business. "Is anybody listening, Bernie? Can you talk?"

"I'm alone on the library extension."

"Very well. If anybody asks you, I called to give you particulars on the divorce suit."

"Right."

"But this is what I really want. Tonight by air mail I'm sending you a check for ten thousand dollars."

"Thanks offering?"

"No. You buy and sell stocks, don't you?"

"I hope so."

"I want you to put that ten thousand to my credit in your brokerage house. Tomorrow, as soon as the divorce goes through, I'm leaving Reno for some place, I don't yet know where. But wherever it is, I'll call you and give you instructions as to what you're to do with the money. Tonight all I want to know is: Can I count on you to carry out my instructions exactly as I give them to you?"

"Now wait a minute, Carrie. Stocks are my business, but after all, I like you. I don't want you to lose your shirt—"

"That's *my* lookout."

"What *is* this, anyway?"

"I don't know yet. I'm not sure it's anything except a brainstorm. But—it may mean a lot to me. I've *got* to have somebody in New York I can trust. Bernie, you'll do this much for me, won't you?"

He thought so long over this that I began to worry about my charges, but at last he said: "I don't like it. I don't like any of it. I can tell from the way you talk you're gambling your money on some kind of tip you expect to get, and there's a special room on the Street where they shear lambs like you. Still, it's your own affair and your own money. All right, send on the money. I'll take care of it."

"Thanks."

■   ■   ■

The next day in court I stammered through my recital of Grant's ungovernable temper, his threats to strike me, and all the other things I was required to tell, and they were all true, so I could swear to them with a perfectly clear conscience. And yet they had so little relation to the real story that it seemed as though I was taking part in a trial that concerned somebody else. Hardly anybody was there, for the Reno courts do not permit the newspapers to treat people as they do in New York, and it only took a short time anyhow. The decree was granted a few minutes after I left court, and then I went over with Mr. Hyde to his office to sign papers. He then turned over to me his own check for the remaining $25,000, shook hands with me, and that seemed to be all.

I walked around to the second-hand dealer's where I had left the car on my way to court. He offered me $750, which I didn't think was enough, considering how little I had driven it, but I was in no mood to argue, so I said all right and he gave me his check. I went over to the bank where I had started a local account and deposited both checks, the one for $25,000 and the one for $750. Then I started back for the hotel. When I came to the bridge over the river I stopped and stood looking down into the water. You are supposed to throw your wedding ring into it as soon as you have your divorce, but I had no wedding ring. What I was thinking about was: What am I going to do about Mr. Holden? I can't marry him, at any rate not now, and yet I have to go with him if I am going to succeed with the stock market operations I have in mind.

Chapter Fifteen

He was waiting for me in the lobby and came up with me to my suite. For the first time in two months he became personal, put his arms around me, took my hat off and ran his fingers through my hair. I sat down on a chair, not the sofa, but he sat down on the arm beside me and continued to lift my hair and let it fall back against my neck. "So. Now you're free."

"Yes."

"How do you prefer to be married?"

"I—don't quite know what you mean."

"I prefer the clerk of the license bureau, myself, but if you want a minister I've made a list of six—all different denominations."

"...Do you mind sitting over there? I have something to say to you."

He looked a little hurt but in a moment crossed over to another chair and sat down. I wanted to be friendly, but I am afraid I sounded very curt and businesslike when I spoke. "I can't marry you today."

"...I had planned on it, Carrie."

"I know. So had I. Anyway, I had taken it for granted. But I'm not ready yet. I'm not readjusted. I want time to think and to know you a little better—under circumstances when I'm not all mixed up inside."

It was all false and phony, and the halting way I said it gave it a sound of sincerity that made me ashamed of it all the more. He looked at me a long time, and then he burst out: "Damn it, Carrie, why do you have to feel this way? I've been counting on you! I have a devil's own time ahead of me, and I've been looking forward to having you with me! I—"

"You may. If you want me."

"Ah!"

"No—don't jump to conclusions. I don't quite mean *that*—or at any rate what I think you have in mind. Off and on, ever since I've known you, you've tried to persuade me to become active in union work, and even offered me positions—if you want me with you couldn't I be your secretary? Won't you need one?"

He was over beside me before I even finished, kissing me, with tears starting out of his eyes. "Would you do that, Carrie? I'll *have* to have one. And if I have you—*I know* I'll win! With that bright little head you have on your shoulders—"

"But mind you, I mean *secretary*. I don't mean— something else."

"If you're with me, do I care what you mean?"

"I'm going to have my own suite, wherever we go, and pay for it—"

"Stop talking, Carrie. I'm too happy to argue."

"But I'm not through yet."

"I am. I know all I want to know."

"If I'm to be your secretary that means I'm a full-fledged unionist—or whatever you call it—"

"Of course you are. You're still a member in good standing of the culinary workers' union—"

"—And I have to know more about what I'm expected to do."

"The little head again. No wonder I love you, Carrie."

"What is this project, anyway?"

"I told you. We're hitting the big industries. The ones that unions so far have been afraid—or unable—really to tackle."

"Which industries?"

"Now that you're my secretary I can tell you. Automobiles. Steel. Rubber. The mass-production industries that employ thousands—hundreds of thousands. They're the future of the labor movement."

"And where do *we* go, you and I?"

"The 'we' sounds sweet, Carrie. First to Detroit."

"Oh—the automobile industry?"

"Yes And guess which plant we tackle first."

"I haven't any idea."

"The toughest of them all—I saw to that. For the moral effect. We play one against the other, but first we move in on Geerlock."

My heart was pounding so that I hardly knew what I was saying when I asked if I could be alone while I packed. However, he noticed nothing and told me to take my time, as we wouldn't leave until five o'clock. He didn't care to fly the northern airlanes at this time of year so we were going by train, and he was in very high spirits when he left me to arrange both compartments. As soon as I had locked the door I darted for the phone and called Mr. Hunt at his office. The call went through in just a few minutes but it seemed a year. "Bernie?"

"Yes, Carrie?"

"Now I've found out what I didn't know last night. As soon as you get my check I want you to sell me short on Geerlock common."

"Geerlock! Carrie, you're crazy! The stock's a buy! It's been zooming since the spring. They're snowed under with orders and—"

"Bernie! Please! I know what I'm doing! And you said you'd do what I—"

"But this is lunacy! You ought to be examined!"

"All right, I'll *get* examined. But will you—"

"I'll do anything you say, but it makes me sick."

"How much margin will you require?"

"On Geerlock? It's now selling at 110—ten points."

"Then my $10,000 will cover me on 1,000 shares—"

"For a couple of weeks, until you're wiped out."

"And how long will it take you to get rid of that amount of stock? I mean, under the SEC rule?"

"The rule is, that if we sell short we can only sell at a price higher than the last previous sale of that stock. But that part's easy. In this market it's no trick to sell short—and go broke. You'll be wiped out so fast—"

"I asked you how long it would take."

"A day, no longer."

"All right, then. As soon as my check arrives, sell."

"I'll sell, but I'm turning green."

"Take some bicarbonate."

■   ■   ■

I sent for my long distance phone bills, for I didn't want them paid by Mr. Hyde. I had just sent the boy down with the money when there came a rap on the door. I opened it, and it was Mr. Bolton. "Just dropped in to say goodbye. How do you feel?"

"Terrible."

"What? You should be gay—think of it, shackles have been struck off your wrists! What's the matter, Carrie?"

"I've just double-crossed a man."

"The candidate for your hand?"

"Yes."

"I knew you'd never marry *that* guy."

"It's a little worse than that. I'm cold-bloodedly using him to further my schemes."

"What schemes?"

"Money."

"You're certainly a mercenary little rat."

"And he's decent and loves me. I feel like hell."

He took both my hands in his, then dropped them and turned away quickly, for he hated to betray that he liked anybody or was anything except a crusty bachelor. But for a moment or two, while he talked, his voice was very soft and he wasn't a crusty bachelor at all. "Carrie, if you really *were* a mercenary little rat and were doing what you say you're doing you'd bore me and I wouldn't waste five minutes on you."

"Oh, I'm doing it, all right."

"You're doing it, but not for the reasons you think. You can deny it all you please, but you're really a young woman in love. You're determined to have that Grant back and you don't care how you do it. I guess you're right. You'll have to lick Agnes before you can do anything else, and all I can say is—all's fair in love, and more power to you. If a labor leader has to be double-crossed, then to hell with him. Cross him and forget him. Look at me now, Carrie."

"...I'm looking."

"Get that man."

"Then you don't—despise me?"

"I just love you—for your cold-blooded little soul and something in your heart that isn't cold...Get that slug and make a man out of him. Promise me?"

"...I'll try."

"Atta girl."

He took my hand and gave me a kind, warm smile and I felt a great deal better.

■   ■   ■

We arrived in Detroit Christmas afternoon and at once went to a small hotel out near the factory. It wasn't much of a place and this surprised me, as previously Mr. Holden had always lived in a very elegant way. But he explained that it would be his headquarters for some time and that it was important that the people he would see feel comfortable there and not self-conscious about coming in, as they might if he went to one of the more fashionable hotels downtown. He gave me permission to go to a better place if I wished, but I decided to stay here. I didn't take a suite. I took a single room with bath, and my reason was that I knew most hotels had rules against their women guests entertaining visitors in a bedroom, and this would be my excuse for not letting Mr. Holden or anybody come up there. I registered as C. Selden, hoping the newspapers would not identify me from that, and thank heaven they didn't.

My room was high up, but he took a suite on the second floor so his visitors could reach it merely by walking up one flight of stairs. I thought at first this was to make it convenient for them, but I soon found out it was also for secrecy. For they merely drifted into the hotel without having to announce themselves at the desk or attract the attention of the elevator boys, and fifty or sixty a day would be in and out without any fuss. My salary was $40 a week. He offered me $60 but I told him $40 was all I would take. I would really have preferred to work for nothing, considering all the circumstances, but as this would have looked very peculiar I accepted $40 and paid my own bills.

I consciously made myself as useful as I could. I handled all phone calls, of which there were hundreds a day, and did all sorts of small errands, kept the callers entertained while he was conferring with two or three of them in the inside room of the suite, kept a record of his expenditures. These were startlingly large. They included the pay of a large number of organizers who were working with him, the expenses of these men, the rent of halls whenever he felt it necessary to hold a large meeting, hiring of automobiles and all sorts of things.

In less than a week I could feel we were embarked on something on a very large scale that was going to mean a fight to the death. All these men who kept coming in and out, "key men," as Mr. Holden called them, from the positions they occupied in the factory, were very grim and terribly in earnest. They had little to say when they were brought in by the organizers and waited their turn to see Mr. Holden, but there was no mistaking the frame of mine they were in. They meant business, and it was very different from the noisy pep meeting we had in Reliance Hall that night when the Karb waitresses got ready to strike.

And yet, try as I would to take some interest in it, since I realized it was important and would soon concern everybody, I remained throughout wholly indifferent to it. All I could think of was the desperate gamble I had undertaken on how it would all turn out. I was on the long distance phone every night talking to Mr. Hunt, and could hardly wait to get the afternoon papers to see what Geerlock common had done in the course of the day. For the first week things went very badly with me. Mr. Hunt made the short sales the day before Christmas while I was on the train at 111, 111⅛ and 111½ in lots of 300, 300 and 400, and then the stock climbed ½ or ¾ a point a day until it was selling for 113. He was frantic. He told me I was half wiped out already and pleaded with me to let him cover before I lost my whole $10,000. My hands would feel like ice every time I thought of it, but I made myself hold on and send him $5,000 more margin. A day or two before New Year's one of our organizers was beaten up by company guards and ejected from the plant, and nine men were fired because they had been seen talking with him. Mr. Holden at once wired the National Labor Relations Board, then jumped in a taxicab, went downtown and gave the story to the newspapers, with a copy of his telegram. The day after that, the item appeared in the papers. That was the first general knowledge, I think, that things were brewing in the Geerlock factory. The day after that, while the market as a whole moved up, Geerlock had a little dash after it, meaning "no change." Once more I felt a throb inside of me, for I felt it was the news of union activity that had caused my stock to sag below the others.

Next day there were more beatings at the factory, and then a representative of the National Board arrived and day after that there was a long interview in the papers with Mr. Beauvais, the president of the company, who said the union was infested with Communists and charged the National Board with trying to run his company, and then went on to say he would fight to the last ditch. "And we'll knock him into it," said Mr. Holden, when he finished reading the paper. "He weighs 250 pounds, so he'll make a fine splash."

The day after that, although the market again moved upward, Geerlock went down a point to 112. When I went up to my room to change for dinner a message was there saying call an operator of a certain number in New York. I called and of course she put me right through to Mr. Hunt. He was quite excited. "Listen, you, what's going on out there anyway?"

"Who's looney now?"

"But, Carrie—baby needs shoes!"

"...It might go down more yet."

"When?"

"Before it goes up. It might sag a little more the next few days and then drop. But if you lose your shirt don't blame me."

The next day, on another rising market, the stock dropped a half point to 111½.

■   ■   ■

The day after New Year's several big union officials arrived from Washington. Except for Mr. Holden they were the first men of their type I had ever seen and I began to understand why the labor movement is much more formidable than most people seem to realize. They were all men of fine presence, with beautiful manners, but that wasn't what struck me about them. Although one or two were only medium size, and some of them were well up

141

in middle age, they all seemed to walk in that same springy way that Mr. Holden walked, and you knew instinctively that they were fighters. In this respect they were exactly like Mr. Holden, and this side of him I could never quite forget, even in his most romantic moments. I don't mean that it repelled me. There was something thrilling about it and yet something a little frightening about it too.

They arrived just before noon and went into a conference with Mr. Holden to which I was not admitted. I had sandwiches and coffee sent up and when I went in to serve them they seemed to know who I was, for they joked with me in a very friendly way. Then men from the factory began to arrive and for an hour or more they were packed in the inside sitting-room so tight I wondered how they could breathe. Then, by threes and fours, they began to leave. Then, around four o'clock, Mr. Holden and the men from Washington all went out very quickly and I was left alone. I knew something was about to happen. I sent down for a paper but there was very little about Geerlock. I turned to the financial page. Geerlock, which had been sagging steadily the last few days, was down to 109. I had about a $2,000 profit. I wondered if I ought to call Mr. Hunt and tell him to cover.

■　　■　　■

About five o'clock I remembered the radio which Mr. Holden always had in his suite, as he was very fond of music. I turned it on. There was music, but then all of a sudden it stopped in the middle and an announcer very excitedly said a meeting was being held that night by Geerlock employees to take a strike vote and it was expected they would all be out by morning.

■　　■　　■

From then on things happened so fast I don't think I could remember all the details even if I tried. Whether it was the first big automobile strike I don't know, but it was the first that *I* had anything to do with, and Mr. Holden directed it with an audacity that took my breath away. Once the

142

blow had been struck he completely abandoned his policy of secrecy and invented a succession of stunts calculated to get him space in the newspapers. The day after the strike started he hired helicopters to drop food supplies to the pickets, on the pretense that the police had placed them in a state of siege. I protested against the cost and pointed out that police were permitting pickets' wives to visit them, or anybody else who had sensible business, and that they could bring food. He laughed and said the helicopters made a better show. Then another day he found a number of GI students who happened to be musicians, called for their cards to make sure they were members of the union, and had them go over and give a concert to serenade the pickets who by now had put up some barricades. Almost every day he thought of something new and the result was that most of the stories in the newspapers were about what the union was doing, with the company's end of it occupying almost no space at all.

Not that the company kept quiet by any means. Mrs. Beauvais called on the governor to declare martial law, and to use troops, and I don't know what all, and in addition to that demanded that the police disperse the pickets with tear bombs, but they didn't. Then he began denouncing Mr. Holden by name and calling him a Communist and saying that such a strike was really sedition against the Government. All this seemed to entertain Mr. Holden hugely, for he would laugh loudly every time he read the paper, and comment on "the stupidity of Capital" in dealing with the public. "Who reads statements?" he wanted to know. "And who believes them? You can see a helicopter. And you can listen to music. And it sounds friendly. Didn't Henry Ford bring a lot of bagpipers into this town once? I've a notion to put them on the payroll, if they have their kilts with them. ...No, it was the King of England that had the bagpipers. Ford had fiddlers. I guess I'll stick to trombones."

Chapter Sixteen

The stock didn't drop when the strike started. It merely sagged another two points, down to 107, and hung there for more than a week. I now had a profit of about $4,000, and I was in an agony of wondering whether I shouldn't cover. But then one day Mr. Beauvais issued another appeal to the governor, saying if the strike went on two more weeks he would be unable to make deliveries on his new model. Mr. Holden became excited when he read this and again had a great deal to say about the stupidity of business executives. "Think of that! Playing right into our hands. Only a fool would make that admission."

The Beauvais appeal was in the morning papers. As soon as I saw it I pleaded business downtown, jumped in a taxi and dashed to a stock broker's office. It had one of the big electrical boards and the light was constantly winking on and off for Geerlock. The stock was sagging steadily until, by the time I got there, it was 103. I rushed back to the hotel, went to my room and called Mr. Hunt. As soon as he answered I said: "Cover."

"But, Carrie, the bottom's dropped out of it. Let it ride! You'll make—"

"Tomorrow the bottom may be in it again." Because by now I had learned that Mr. Holden moved fast when he started and for all I knew the strike might be settled that afternoon. "How long before closing time?"

"Two hours."

"All right. As long as it drops let it ride. At the least upturn, cover. And no matter what it does, cover today. Don't leave me short for tomorrow morning's market."

"Is that a hint for *my* benefit?"

"No. I don't know anything and nobody does. But I've made something and I don't want to lose it by hanging on too long."

It was after lunch when I got back to Mr. Holden. He was very pleased that he had been able to rent a new Geerlock, a display car. He went out to have his picture taken in it, surrounded by the GI band, so he could release it to the newspapers with a story telling what a fine car it was and how the company ought to settle so they could manufacture it. Shortly after he went out a telegram was delivered to me. It was from Mr. Hunt. He had covered at 102 to 103. Clear of commissions and interest, I had a profit of nearly $8,000.

▪ ▪ ▪

Nothing happened that day or for a week or two. The men continued to hold the shops, Mr. Holden continued to put on his stunts and Mr. Beauvais continued to give out statements. There were several clashes outside the factory gates. Men kept coming in and going out of the hotel and Mr. Holden began to show signs of the strain. The stock continued to sag until it was down near 100 and I kept kicking myself that I could have made more by doing what Mr. Hunt said, but I kept reminding myself of something I had read somewhere, that more money is lost in the stock market by hanging on for the last dollar of profit than in any other way. But then, almost before I knew it, I was in the market again, for Mr. Holden happened to mention one day that they were moving in on Trent, another factory in Detroit, and I repeated my operation, this time making $3,000. And then he mentioned casually what was going on in other places, particularly the steel mills, and next thing I knew I was juggling four or five stocks at the same time, making money on them but becoming more and more nervous and less and less watchful of the Geerlock situation, which was the main thing we were concerned with.

So I was caught napping one day when a call came in for him. He made a memorandum while he was talking, then handed it to me and began putting on his coat. The memorandum gave the number of a room in one of the downtown hotels. "That's where I can be reached—but *only* if it's important."

His face was set but he seemed exultant somehow. He started out, then came back to me and, as nobody was there, gave me a little kiss. Then he whispered: "I think Beauvais is going to settle."

Then he was gone, and I let ten or fifteen precious minutes slip by, stupidly thinking how glad I was that the thing was all over, when suddenly I woke up. How I ever got up to my room I don't know, but it seemed an eternity before I had the telephone in my hand and got the call put through and finally had Mr. Hunt on the line. "Bernie, how much of a credit have I with you now?"

"Hold the line, Carrie, I'll look it up."

I fairly screamed at him: "No! Don't look it up! Don't waste that much time! Bernie, are you listening?"

"And how."

"Buy Geerlock for me, Bernie! Start *now*! Buy on margin up to every dollar I have on deposit with you! Have you got it?'

"I'm calling our floor man now."

"Buy Geerlock! Every share you can get hold of for me!"

■   ■   ■

The joint statement over the names of Mr. Beauvais and Mr. Holden was given out at four-thirty. It called only for union recognition, all questions of wages and hours to be referred later to a board of arbitration. The men marched out at five o'clock, preceded by their band and met by their wives and families in a very joyous reunion. Mr. Holden returned around six in very high spirits and all ready to take me out to some fashionable place for dinner. He wanted to dress and really celebrate. But the settlement had been arrived at after the New York Market closed and until I knew what my stock was going to do I didn't trust myself with him or anybody else. I told him the reaction from the strain had given me a splitting headache and that I would have to go to my room. I went up there and called Mr. Hunt but he had left his office. Around six-thirty a telegram was delivered. I opened it and it was a long wire from Mr. Hunt, telling me where I stood. I had a credit of $31,000, which included the original $10,000 I had put up, the additional $5,000 margin I had sent, the $8,000 I had made on Geerlock, the $3,000 I had made on Trent and various amounts I had made on other deals, of course with commissions and other charges deducted. This afternoon for my account, on a ten-point margin, there had been bought for my account 3,100 shares of Geerlock common in lots of 300 to 500 shares, at prices ranging from 101 to 102½. It was easy to see that my buying had run the price up nearly two points while my order was being executed.

I had dinner sent up but could eat nothing. I changed into pajamas, went to bed and tried to sleep. By midnight I was up walking around the room. I made myself lie down again but was still awake when the sky began to grow light.

■   ■   ■

Next thing I knew the phone was ringing and it was the middle of the morning. "New York calling."

"Put them on."

It was Mr. Hunt and the moment he spoke my name I could hear the excitement in his voice. "Carrie!"

"Yes, Bernie?"

"Baby, you've cleaned up. The stock opened at 102, ran up to 105 in the first half-hour, it's still climbing—and what do I do now?"

"Let me think. Give me a minute to think."

I thought and thought and then came to the conclusion it was a market question entirely and that I had better leave it to him. "Bernie?"

"Yes?"

"I don't know how high it's going to go. Can't you watch it for me and then—"

"You bet I can, Carrie. I'll let it zoom and when it slacks a little I'll close you out."

"But today, Bernie. Don't wait."

"Trust me, Carrie."

I got up, went in the bedroom and ran the water into the tub. I had just got it when the phone rang again and I answered. I was all dripping with water and had only a towel around me, but it was Mr. Hunt back on the line. "I've closed you out, baby. It staggered a little and I didn't like the look of it. You can never tell how high they'll bounce on a rally like that. So I went after it while it was still good.

147

You're out at 108 to 110, average about 109. I'll give you the exact figures by wire."

"Thanks. Many thanks."

"*And* thanks. I was on the bandwagon, baby. I cleaned up, hanging right onto your skirts."

"Oh, I'm glad of that."

"Some skirts."

I got back in the bathtub and tried to figure. As well as I could make out, I had made something more than $20,000 on the deal. Counting what I had made before, it left me over $40,000 for my stay in Detroit. When I had finished bathing I went to the phone and rang Mr. Holden. "If you feel like some lunch, now I think we'll celebrate."

"You bet we'll celebrate. I'll meet you in the lobby."

■　　　■　　　■

The rest of that winter was one mad jumble of trains, hotels, strikes, meetings and worry. On account of his success with Geerlock Mr. Holden was made a sort of general supervisor and moved about from one place to another as he was needed. After we left Detroit he concentrated on steel mills and we went first to Chicago, then into Indiana and finally to Pittsburgh, where the plan was to move in on Penn-Duquesne, one of the large independents. I made about $10,000 during these hectic days but I was curtailing my operations more and more. For one thing, the nervous strain was becoming so great I wasn't sure I could stand it, and for another thing, some instinct told me I had ridden a great run of luck and was about due for a fall. I dreaded that. I had made enough money to pay back Mrs. Harris every cent I had taken from her, and still have enough to live on for years. Or I could even travel, something I had always secretly hoped I would be able to do, in order to broaden myself.

So I determined to return to New York. My decision was hastened, perhaps, by the increasing difficulty of my relations with Mr. Holden. Almost nightly now he was making love to me and insisting that we get married. Then, also, he was becoming more and more puzzled at my attitude, and hurt by it, for which I could hardly blame him, considering everything. But I wished above everything else to avoid a big farewell scene with him and so pretended that I wasn't saying goodbye at all. I merely said I had been called to New York to wind up some details of my financial settlement with the Harrises and told him I would call him by long distance very night. This, I am a little ashamed to say, I fully intended to do, for I had made a little $1,000 commitment against Penn-Duquesne, on the short side, I mean, and I wanted to keep track of things so I would know how to handle it. He suspected nothing. He rode with me to the airport, for by this time I went everywhere by plane, and was very affectionate and urged me to get back as soon as I could. "I've a hard nut to crack this time, Carrie. I need you."

"I'll call you—every night."

"I'll be standing by—every night at twelve sharp."

■　　　■　　　■

I reached Newark at one o'clock. I took a taxi at once to the hotel where I had reserved a suite. Then I rushed down to my bank, which I hadn't visited in more than three months, and went over both my balances there, the checking and the savings. Most of my money was on deposit with Mr. Hunt, but I still had several thousand here from the original $25,000 I had deposited before I left New York. As soon as I had checked over my books with them I drew $5,000 cash and took a taxi over to Fifth Avenue. The rest of the afternoon I spent buying clothes, for I wanted to look quite smart when I made my appearance at Harris, Hunt and Harris the next morning. I looked up Miss Eubanks, the lady who had been so helpful to me before, and she outfitted me again.

When I told her what I wanted she at once advised black. This I agreed to, as I had never had a black dress, and I was quite excited to know how I would look in it. She picked out a model made of sheer wool and I loved it. It made me look slim, but it was very severe and I wanted something to relieve it a little. But when I mentioned this Miss Eubanks became quite upset and said the whole point of the dress would be lost if I added anything to it whatever. She then lectured me on the need for simplicity, which was something I always tried to remember but sometimes forgot. So I took it as it was, and she helped me pick hat, shoes and stockings to go with it, as well as a smart black handbag. Then we picked out two evening dresses, one light blue, the other cream white, and again they were completely simple and unadorned.

When we got through picking the shoes and stockings to go with these it was nearly five o'clock and then I got to the main thing that was on my mind. I wanted her to go with me to pick out a fur coat, and as I already spent so much money with her store I thought they might let her off. So she spoke to the head of her department and he said all right and she called me one of the leading furriers to make sure they would be open when we got there. So then we took a taxi and went down there. But next door to the furrier's was a perfume place, and before we proceeded to buy the coat I dashed in and bought some perfume I had always loved and had never been able to afford. It cost $25 for a little bottle, and I would have taken it if it had cost $50.

At the furrier's they brought us into a private room and paraded models in front of me. Finally I decided on a mink coat, so dark and so beautifully made that it looked like sable. Miss Eubanks advised the three-quarter length, as she said it was smarter and more becoming to me. It cost $2,500 and I paid cash and took it with me. I asked Miss Eubanks to come around to the hotel with me for dinner and when we got there the package from her store had been delivered and we spent the next two hours trying on my things and even after she had gone home that night, which was around ten o'clock, I tried them on all over again and finally stood in front of the long mirror in the bathroom door in my new black street dress, big black hat and beautiful mink coat for more than an hour. I hated to go to bed.

■　　　■　　　■

Harris, Hunt and Harris were in a gigantic office building on Broad Street, one of the places I had gone into at the time I was considering a restaurant business of my own downtown. They occupied one whole floor. I had not phoned Mr. Hunt I was coming, as I could not quite resist the temptation to burst in on him as a big surprise. But when I stepped out of the elevator and gave my name to the girl at the window she looked up quickly and reached for her telephone. I had barely sat down when a gentleman appeared who said he was Mr. Hunt's secretary and invited me inside. "Mr. Hunt stepped out, Mrs. Harris, but he's in the building and I'll have him located at once."

He opened a door and began leading me through a very large room with bright lights and rows and rows of desks where people were busily working. A stir went over the place as soon as I appeared. Nobody stared but I could feel that I was a object of great curiosity and that they were all aware of me, from the girls, who started talking to each other with an elaborate appearance of casualness, to the men, who kept shooting little glances at me over papers they pretended to examine.

That is, all except one. Behind a desk at the far end of the room where I would have to pass him, sat Grant, and I could tell that he hadn't seen me or noticed any of the commotion I had caused. My heart stood still when I saw him and I almost turned around and ran out. However, I kept following the secretary, and then suddenly I wanted to cry. Because he looked so insignificant there, with a green shade over his eyes and a pipe in his mouth, writing something on a piece of paper. Most of the sunburn was gone and he looked sallow and seedy. It flashed through my mind what he had once said about being a slave, and I wished he would at least take off the green eyeshade, which depressed me most of all.

But I kept sailing bravely along, and then I remembered my perfume. As I passed his desk I opened my coat quickly so he could get a good whiff of it as I went by. He looked up and our eyes met. "Oh, hello!" I said, just as gaily as though nothing had ever happened between us at all. Then I zipped through a glass door marked "Mr. Hunt," and the secretary was bowing me into a big leather chair. But all I could think of was the amazed look on Grant's face, and

I began fumbling in my handbag so I wouldn't show how much I wanted to cry.

■   ■   ■

The secretary went and in a moment there came a rap on the door. I tried to look casual and said, "Come in." Grant was standing there, the green shade still over his eyes, acting terribly nervous and not quite looking me in the eye. I struggled for control so I could act naturally, and yet it was a second or so before I heard myself say: "Well! How have you been?"

"Very well, thank you."

But he sounded shaky and queer. I held out my hand and he took it. "And how have you been?"

"Quite well, thank you."

"You're looking well."

"Thank you."

"And you're certainly a success."

"Oh, am I?"

"A Wall Street celebrity, I should say. The whole place has practically suspended activity trying to find out what you're going to do next."

"I didn't know I was that important."

"Oh, you're pretty important...You've become prominent in the labor movement, Bernie tells me."

"Oh—I keep in touch."

"I got interested in it myself once."

"Oh, yes. I seem to remember, now you speak of it."

"I guess I'm not cut out for large affairs, though. It never occurred to me it could be used as a basis for market speculation."

He sounded a little bitter as he said this, and I replied: "I'm afraid you disapprove of my career in the market."

"Oh, no. I'm merely learning things. What's your part in the movement?"

"I'm afraid I haven't any just at present. I was a sort of traveling secretary."

"Oh."

He licked his lips once or twice as though they were dry, and I knew he was dying to ask about Mr. Holden, but

I volunteered nothing. There was a long uncomfortable pause and then he said suddenly: "What name are you using now, Carrie?"

This caught me wholly by surprise. I had been half enjoying the foolish talk we had been carrying on but now the same icy feeling began to creep around my heart that I had had in the last days before he left me. "...Why— that's something I hadn't quite got around to. The court gave me permission to resume my maiden name, and traveling around that's what I use. But on my bank accounts and in my business transactions I'm still using yours. Why?"

"Oh, nothing. I just wanted to know."

"Nothing was said about it in the agreement that was drawn up."

"No, I saw to that."

"If my use of your name bothers you—"

"Not at all. In fact, it's not on my account I raised the question. But mother—"

"Oh, 'mother' again!"

"...I guess I shouldn't have brought it up."

"So after the way you treated me, after you let that woman wrap you around her finger like some kind of worm—"

"We don't have to go into that."

"Oh, yes, we do! After all that, all you can think of to say to me now is that you don't want me to use your name because that simpleton finds it a little inconvenient to have a second Mrs. Harris around to spoil her solitary eminence! Well, I'm *going* to use your name!"

"It's quite all right, Carrie."

"But for a reason you don't know anything about yet. *I don't know my own name!*"

"You—? What did you say?"

"That's something the newspapers didn't find out about me, with *all* their snooping around. I don't *know* my name! And while I was perfectly welcome to use my foster-parents' name, yours is the first name that was ever legally mine. And I'm going to use it! The court didn't say I *had* to use my former name. It only said I could if I chose. I choose. I'm going to use your name. Not that I like it. But it'll do until I get another which, praise god, may not be long now."

153

This last slipped out on me, for I truly hadn't given Mr. Holden a thought all morning. But I was so bitter over the whole discussion that I couldn't help saying it. He wheeled around, his eyes blazing, caught my hand and tried to jerk me up so that I would be standing, facing him. "What do you mean by that?"

I sat where I was and slowly twisted my hand out of his grasp before I answered. "What I mean by it is none of your business. You left me, you let your mother pay me to get a divorce, and now I'm free. This was your choice, not mine. Isn't that true?"

I looked at him when I said this and his eyes dropped. He walked around the office two or three times, picking up things and putting them down, and then abruptly turned and walked out.

Chapter Seventeen

A minute or two after that Mr. Hunt breezed in, kissed me and was perfectly lovely, but the meeting with Grant had taken all the fun out of my nice surprise. I explained briefly the reason for my strained manner, and switched at once to what I had come there about. I told him I was ready to pay back Mrs. Harris what I had taken from her, shut him up when he began to protest, and said I wanted him to have her at my hotel promptly at eleven o'clock the next morning, to have the money with him in cash, and then I would wash my hands of everything called Harris, and before many days were out even get rid of the name itself. When he saw I was not to be shaken in my decision he stopped arguing and got down to other matters he had to straighten out, chiefly concerning the large balance I was carrying with him and what he was to do with it.

However, we were interrupted by the entrance of the secretary, who told him Mrs. Jerome was waiting to see him, and he excused himself a minute. When he came back he was laughing. "Baby, are you a sensation! When that woman found out you were in here she just camped down, and a fat chance I can get rid of her until she shakes your money-clutching paw."

"I don't want to meet her."

"You *did* meet her, at my house."

"Oh—yes, I remember her. I can't see her! I'm not in the humor! I—this thing has upset me and I don't want to see *anybody!*"

"Carrie! Just for a minute—then I'll ride you uptown in the car and we'll wind up our business at lunch. Listen! This woman meant dough to me."

So he brought her in. She was a big fat woman with gray hair and I remembered her from Mrs. Hunt's cocktail party. She began gushing over me and inviting me to spend the weekend at her place on Long Island. I said I had made engagements for the week-end. She became so insistent that, to get her out of there, Mr. Hunt said he wanted to show us his shop as he called it. I said I had to go, but he reminded me he was driving uptown and there was nothing I could do but tag along with them, though what there would be to see I couldn't for the life of me imagine. As he went out the glass door I looked toward Grant's desk but he was gone.

■　　　■　　　■

There was a big electrical board in the place but that was an old story to me now and I sat on the edge of a desk while he explained it to her. It was a desk belonging to a "customer's man," as they call it in the brokerage offices. The board is a great big affair which occupies one whole wall and has all the stocks listed, with the numbers winking on and off in lights as the sales are made. Some distance out from the board are chairs where people sit and watch the quotations, but directly in front of it is the battery of customers' men, each with a separate desk on which are two telephones, one for incoming calls and the other direct to the floor of the Exchange. As the orders come in these men accept them, then phone them to the floor man at the Exchange, who executes them. There were four desks in front of this board and at three of them men were busy at their phones. However, the man on whose desk I was sitting had gone off somewhere. A secretary came up, looked around, then tucked a yellow slip into the blotting pad. I don't remember being curious about it and must have glanced at it mechanically. But I felt my mouth go hot from fury at what I saw.

It was a "sell" order—a printed blank with spaces for name, date, stock, number of shares, etc. In lead pencil at the top was the name "Mrs. Harwood Harris," and the Harwood was underscored three times. That was evidently to keep Mrs. Harwood Harris separate from the other Mrs. Harris, who was myself. The order was for 1,000 shares of Penn-Duquesne, and off on the side in compliance with the SEC rule was written the word "short."

Anybody could see that what Mr. Hunt had done was tip Mrs. Harris off to what I was doing in stocks, for it was only yesterday morning that I had phoned him from Pittsburg to sell a small block of this stock for me. And while I was really a sort of friendly enemy with him, I couldn't help feeling that this was a pretty dirty trick. So when he drifted over for a minute while Mrs. Jerome was examining one of the tickers I pointed to the "sell" order and said; "I don't think that was very nice of you."

"Listen, baby, her affairs had got to a certain point. Do you know what I mean? Something had to be done."

"I would think you could have found some other way to do it."

"I'd been trying for a year to find other ways and there weren't any...I certainly hope you're riding a winner again. She's in deep. That's only one little hunk of it."

He went back to Mrs. Jerome. And then suddenly a perfectly fiendish idea entered my mind to get back at Mrs. Harris. If there were some way I could persuade Mr. Holden to leave Penn-Duquesne alone instead of calling a strike the stock wouldn't go down. It would go up—and my lovely mother-in-law would be ruined.

Suddenly I became very sweet and interested in everything, particularly Mrs. Jerome. I joined her at the ticker and said; "I've been thinking over my engagements, Mrs. Jerome, and I believe I could fit you in. If the invitation is still open I'd love to spend the weekend with you." For I thought: If everything goes the way I hope, a weekend with Society is exactly the way I'll want to celebrate.

She was delighted, gave me directions for getting down to Great Neck, and said she would meet me at the train and that I was to bring "rough, outdoorsy" things. She went then, and Mr. Hunt took me around to his bank and introduced me. I signed the necessary cards and they started an account in my name with the credit I had with him. We then went to lunch at a little restaurant down near the Battery and then he drove me uptown. He kept laughing over my social eminence. "Carrie, I'm proud of you! Monday you'll be on the Society page. She *always* consents—graciously, of course, and only after the newspapers call *her*—to reveal her week-end activities. Are you a success!"

But all I could think of was that I had to get hold of Mr. Holden.

∎   ∎   ∎

I didn't even wait to take off my mink coat and hang it up before I called him at his hotel in Pittsburgh. The report came back that he was out. I left word that he was to call me and gave the hotel number. Then I sat there and waited. Then I sent down for some magazines, to get my mind off it, but when they came up I threw them aside and began walking around, for I still didn't know what I was going to say to him, even when he called. Then after awhile I realized that I *did* know what I was going to say to him, and had known all along. I was going to say I was lonesome for him, and try to entice him away from Pittsburgh by practically promising myself to him. For I knew the labor situation very well by then, and I was pretty sure if he didn't conduct the Penn-Duquesne strike there was no other leader who would be able to. As soon as I admitted this to myself a struggle began inside of me. I kept telling myself I would be starting something I might be sorry for afterwards and that the ruination of Mrs. Harris, after all, was hardly a sufficient reason and certainly not a very creditable reason, for taking a step which might affect my whole life. It didn't do any good. She had become a mania with me now, and now that she was so nearly within my grasp there was nothing I would stop at to satisfy what I felt against her.

The phone rang and I fairly leaped for it. It was the Pittsburgh operator to tell me that on the call to a Mr. Evan Holden, Mr. Holden had not yet returned to his hotel but that they would keep after him. That went on all afternoon and part of the night. Then along toward midnight I realized it had been a couple of hours since the last report. I picked up the phone and put the call in again. I had hardly begun to march around when the phone rang and it was the Pittsburgh operator. "On that call to Mr. Evan Holden, Mr. Holden has checked out of the hotel without leaving any address where he can be reached."

■   ■   ■

It was nearly ten o'clock when I woke up the next morning. I hurriedly bathed and dressed, and then to save time I ordered my breakfast sent up. But just as it arrived the desk called to say Mr. Hunt was downstairs. I had the waiter wheel it in the bedroom and leave it there, so I would not have to ask Mr. Hunt to sit there and watch while I gulped down coffee and eggs. Besides, I suddenly didn't feel like eating anything.

He came in, shook hands, and at once opened a large briefcase which he carried with him and took out a long sealed envelope to which a receipt was attached with a rubber band. He held it out to me. "Here is the money—fifty one-thousand-dollar bills. Now Carrie, I want to ask you once more: Are you sure you want to do this? Fifty thousand dollars is a lot of money. Some day you may need it. You can still change your mind if you want to. She doesn't know why you've sent for her. I merely told her to be here and said it was important. I guess I deliberately misled her a little. I let her think you're meditating some kind of legal action—"

"That's impossible. The agreement took care of that."

"Of course, but the way is still clear for you to rant and rave a little and pretend that's what you wanted—and still say nothing about the money. If you think anything of my advice you'll keep it."

"I don't know what I want to do." Because after the chance I had seen yesterday to get back at her, merely handing the money back didn't seem any satisfaction at all. And the envelope, all stuffed full of money, looked so thick and lovely I hated the idea of giving it to her. And yet I had sent for her and had to have it out with her or go insane, and the money seemed the only possible excuse for what I had to say.

I slid the receipt out from under the rubber band. "Do I sign here?"

He handed me his fountain pen. I signed and handed him the pen and the receipt. Then I quickly pitched the envelope up on the mantelpiece.

"You'd better count it."

"I'll take your word for it." Because I knew if I ever felt that money between my fingers I couldn't bear to part with it.

He put the receipt in his briefcase and just then the phone rang. He looked at his watch. "That may be Grant. I meant to tell you. She insisted that he be here."

"That's all right."

The desk said Mr. Harris was in the lobby and I told them to send him up. He came in with a hunted, hangdog look that I hated. We all sat there for a few minutes looking at our watches until I couldn't stand it any longer and asked them if I could fix them something to drink. Mr. Hunt shook his head, Grant didn't even answer. Then he looked at me for the first time since he had been there and almost spit at me: "What's between mother and this man Holden, anyway?"

"Why—I don't know, I'm sure."

"I think you do. And what's between him and you, by the way, too?"

"That's none of your business."

"I'm warning you now that I've taken about all off that guy I'm going to take."

"Very well, but I wish you'd make up your mind what you have against him. Because your mother is one thing, I'm something else."

"Not necessarily."

At this moment Mr. Hunt said, "Children, children," and we became silent again. The significance of the threats about Mr. Holden did not dawn on me then, but in a minute or two I was to find out what lay back of them. The desk called promptly at eleven and said a Mrs. Harris was in the lobby, and I told them to send her up. But when she knocked and I opened the door to let her in who should be with her but Mr. Holden.

■　　■　　■

I was so surprised that when she took me in her arms and kissed me I let her, although I had fully intended to refuse even to shake hands. He patted my arm, and apparently was not aware there was anything unusual going on. When I brought them in, though, and he saw Grant, he was on his guard at once. He spoke affably but I could see his quick glance shoot around at all of us. Grant nodded to him coldly, and then I introduced him to Mr. Hunt, who seemed as much surprised at his presence there as I was. Then we all sat down and he took out a cigarette and began tapping it on his finger. Then he looked at me and said: "Well. I had no idea I was going to wind up here when Mrs. Harris called me this morning, Carrie."

"Oh, you're back at the Wakefield?"

"M'm. For a day or two."

"I didn't know that."

I was just saying things that meant nothing. I wanted to ask him how he could leave Penn-Duquesne, and what he was doing here, and what she had said to him, and a lot of other things, but I couldn't do it before all the others, and I couldn't quite make myself ask him to step into the bedroom. It was all going differently from the way I had planned, and I had some panicky instinct that she had got the jump on me, but there was nothing I could do but begin. I turned to her. "Mrs. Harris, I've asked you here to discuss a little matter of business."

"Yes, Carrie? I love to talk business."

Her voice was like honey, but her eyes had the old familiar glassy look, and I wanted to back down, to say never mind, that it was nothing important and I preferred not to mention it. But I knew I had to go on. "But before we get to the business part there are one or two matters I want to take up with you."

160

"Why, certainly, Carrie. Speak freely. After all, you're among friends...What matters?"

"...How you broke up my marriage, for instance."

I sounded all muffled and frightened, and she laughed. "Now, Carrie, you're joking."

"No, I'm not joking."

My voice came back when I said that, and I ripped it out as though I meant it, and stood up facing her. And she came back the same way, shrill and loud, the way she always talked when she got angry. "That'll be enough of that, young woman. I've been expecting it, I know just what you're up to—"

"You don't know what I'm up to!"

"Yes, I do, and I warn you that anything of that kind that you attempt is going to have most unpleasant consequences." She stood up, then, and faced me, and the two of us were in the center of the room like a pair of fighting hens. Grant said something quickly, but she paid no attention to him, and went on, shaking her finger at me. "I'm all ready for you. I'm quite prepared to prove that you never had a marriage to break up, that you deceived and betrayed my son even on his wedding day and before. I've taken good care to bring your paramour with me—and we'll let *him* tell who broke up your marriage."

She turned dramatically to Mr. Holden, and I don't know what she thought he was going to say, but he just laughed. "Be your age, Agnes, if that's why you insisted I come here with you. I broke up no marriage. And I'm not her paramour—worse luck."

At this Grant jumped up, his fists clenching and unclenching. "That's a lie, Holden. You've been traveling around the country with her, stopping at the same hotels—"

Mr. Holden looked up then, with such a queer look on his face that Grant stopped. "Mr. Harris, I understand your anger, but I don't respect it. Only two people can break up a marriage, the husband and the wife. I can speak for the wife, in this case. I tried with every ounce that was in me to get her to come with me, to leave you, because I loved her and I thought you were no good. I tried without avail. She didn't break up the marriage. That leaves you. Am I right?"

161

Grant tried to answer him and couldn't, and slumped down in his chair again, twice as hangdog-looking as he had been before. Mr. Holden then added: "I have never been her lover, in the hotels or any other place—though I've tried to be, I say to my credit. I don't care to hear any more out of you on this subject."

Grant began to shake and put his fingers in his ears even while Mr. Holden was talking, so it was embarrassing to look at him, but Mrs. Harris wasn't done yet. She ran over to Mr. Holden and screamed: "How about those stock deals? How about those stock deals?"

"What stock deals?"

"You can't deny it! The stock deals you and she have been putting over! Do you mean to say you made her all that money—*just to be nice to her?*"

"I've never bought a share of stock, and I don't think Carrie would know one from a hard-boiled egg—"

"*What?* Why, Bernie handled the deals! He—"

"Oh, mother, shut up, shut up—let Carrie finish and let's get out of here, or I'll go mad!" Grant sounded as though he was in agony, but I only half heard what he said. I was watching Mr. Holden, who had turned around suddenly toward Mr. Hunt. He then turned slowly around to me, and by the look on his face I knew he realized that what she said was true, that I had been dealing in stocks, and that he knew why. Mrs. Harris kept on screaming, but he paid no attention to her. He went over the window and stood looking out at the sky. Then he turned to me. "That's why you wanted to be my secretary, Carrie?"

"...Yes."

I felt sick when I said it, and nobody spoke, and he kept looking at me. "That you could use for profit—something that was meant for glory? That men fought for, and bled for, and—believed in?"

"...Yes."

Mrs. Harris began to scream again. "She made thousands—*thousands*," but he sat down again, and motioned her to be quiet. "No more, Agnes, if you don't mind. I had a flower in my heart when I came in here, and it's not there any more...Give me a minute. I'll mourn my dead, and be off."

He sat staring ahead of him, and nobody said anything. Mr. Hunt came over and patted my cheeks with his handkerchief. Tears were pouring out of my eyes so I could hardly see.

■   ■   ■

Mr. Holden got up then, walked heavily over to the table, picked up his hat and went out. I took the handkerchief and hid my face in it. After a long time I felt Mr. Hunt tapping me on the shoulder. "Somebody's out there. Do you want me to go, or—"

"I'll go."

I went out in the hall. Mr. Holden was standing there. He closed the door, walked over toward the elevators, and stood leaning against the wall. "...I couldn't leave you that way, Carrie."

I went over and took his hand. "No—not that way."

"Why did you do it, Carrie?"

"I—I had to pay her back. What I took from her. I—I just had to."

"Well—I could have known it was something with a little spirit to it."

"I couldn't see that it hurt anyone—"

"It didn't. Not Labor, certainly...But—there was no love in it. Or you would have told me."

I began to cry again at that, and he took me in his arms, and held me until I was quiet. I wanted to tell him it wasn't true, that there *was* love in it, but I couldn't. "...Goodbye, Carrie."

"Goodbye."

He pushed the button for the elevator, and we stood there waiting for the car. "I hope you're not involved with Penn-Duquesne, Carrie. They've settled."

"They've—*what?*"

"I see you *are* involved. You'd better do something quick. They've settled—a few cents increase, and a union shop, given us which was all we hoped for. They, as well as some others. It'll be announced to-morrow. We were on it all day yesterday. I got your message, but I took the sleeper. I wanted to surprise you. And then—this frantic call from Agnes this morning. And now—this."

The car came, he got in, and sadly blew me a kiss. I went back, and I swear I wasn't thinking about revenge or anything. But as I came in the room, I heard Mrs. Harris say: "—From that alone you can tell what kind of character she is. Well—a waitress, what can you expect?"

Penn-Duquesne shot through my mind, and I walked through to the bedroom, wondering if I could be horrible enough to ruin her, now that the opportunity was right in my hand. All I had to do was ask them to leave, and say nothing, and she would be wiped out when the stock shot up on the news Mr. Holden had just told me, and I knew from Mr. Hunt she was heavily involved. But just about that time I noticed my breakfast on the wagon, with the covers still on it, where the waiter had put it. And then, all of a sudden, I knew what I was going to do. I went back, sat down, and said brightly: "Now!"

"Yes, Carrie. We've had so many distractions."

Mrs. Harris was her old smiling self again, and I smiled right back and said: "Now, Agnes, you may serve my breakfast."

"I—*what!* And how dare you call me by my first name?"

"I call you by your first name as is customary, for now you're going to be my servant. For one breakfast only, but for that long you're going to be a waitress, as I was once, and I'm going to call you by your first name."

Grant got up and began helping her into her coat. "I don't see any need to prolong this any longer, Mother."

"No—this is simply absurd."

"It is my intention, Agnes, to give you a very handsome tip—fifty thousand dollars, as a matter of fact, the money you paid me to get my divorce from Grant. But for tips I expect service."

"My dear, I'm not accustomed to serving breakfasts for trifles like fifty thousand dollars."

I let her get clear to the door before I made my next remark, which was: "Then perhaps your commitment in Penn-Duquesne may make you feel differently."

She stopped, turned pale and stared at me. But I continued to speak in a cool and casual way: "It's an excellent stock for speculation purposes, and I compliment you on your judgment in selecting it. The only trouble is, it's erratic. There's only one person in this room today who knows what that stock is going to do. I've taken the trouble to find out, solely for your benefit. I can tell you or not. It's entirely up to you."

Grant had stopped and kept looking from one to the other of us like some big St. Bernard dog. But she seemed to get ten years older all in a few seconds, and then she came over to me and leaned close, and spoke in a terrible whisper: "Carrie, tell me, what do you know about that stock? Yes, I've treated you very badly, but only because—Grant means so much to me. Now—let's be friends. The stock, Carrie— *what do you know about it?*"

"You may serve my breakfast, Agnes."

"...Yes. Anything. Anything!"

"Yes *what*, Agnes?"

"Yes, Mrs. Harris."

Chapter Eighteen

The picture of that next few minutes will remain in my memory a great many years, I think. Of Grant staring at her as though he couldn't believe she would do such a thing. Of Mr. Hunt sitting on the sofa, fingering his moustache, his eyes shining, the color creeping up in his cheeks until his whole face was crimson. Of Mrs. Harris, like the middle-aged woman that she really was, her hands shaking so badly she couldn't break the eggs, and almost spilling the orange juice over me in her agitation. And of myself, sitting there munching ice cold toast, which was all I could get down, drinking my revenge and yet trying to appear calm and cool.

■   ■   ■

She was just pouring the coffee when Grant leaped at her. He grabbed her with one hand, her coat with the other, and began hustling her out of the door. "Get out of here!"

he kept whispering at her, but in a rasping way, as though he could hardly restrain his fury. "Get out of here! Get out of here!" He opened the door, and kept jerking her along even when they were out in the hall.

Then Mr. Hunt jumped up. "All right, baby, you've done it. You've harpooned her, up to the hilt. Now—that stock! Give it to me quick. Remember, I'm aboard that deal, too."

"Cover."

He hardly waited for me to finish before he dashed out. I got up to put the coffee cup back on the tray. When I turned around Grant was standing there, still panting. He closed the door and started over to me, his eyes dancing in an almost inhuman way. I backed away from him, but he grabbed me. "Carrie!...You've done it! You've set me free!"

He began kissing me then, but I was still so surprised I didn't give any response, and then he threw himself on the sofa and began pounding on the cushions with his fists. "Don't you suppose I knew what she was—what she did to us, and all the rest of it? Don't you think I hated myself, that I let her use me, make a fool out of me, torture me! Of course she broke up our marriage, and I knew she was doing it, and knew how she was doing it and why—*but her will was stronger than mine!* I couldn't go up against her—nobody can. You've no idea what she's like. And I was doing all sorts of things to break loose—starting unions, trying to break the System—"

"Marrying me."

"Yes!—and I did something that time. *You* went up against her and you made her knuckle. I could have jumped up and yelled, like some kid at a football game. It—broke something. I could feel it snap. I was free! Think of that— she's gone and gambled my money in some stupid stock deal—and I don't care! *I don't care!*"

He came over and looked at me. Then he touched me, the reverent way you touch something to make sure it's there. "I know now what you meant," he said, still in a kind of trance—"what you meant that night. That night when I asked you to marry me, and you said I didn't say anything about love. I didn't know what love meant. No, I never loved you. Not then. Not until now—when I saw you fasten your will on her and make her bend to it. Oh, yes—now it's different. Now everything's different."

He disappeared into the bedroom for a minute or two, then he came out and laughed. For the first time since we had been married, almost, he was the old Grant, the one I remembered from the walk we took together, when we had hooked little fingers together and the cop had told us not to mind him. "Sorry, Carrie. I've—I've been through hell, and I'm a little off my nut."

■　　■　　■

I desperately wanted to run into his arms and make up, but I didn't. I got up and wheeled the breakfast tray out into the hall, and when I came back I said: "Well, it's all very well for you to turn around and say you're sorry, or whatever it is that you mean—but I can't forget quite that easily."

He nodded, very seriously. "I know. I've got some ground to win back. Don't worry, I'll do it. I told Bernie out in the hall just now he could cross me off his damned payroll and from now on I start."

"Start what, may I ask?"

"My Indians."

"How? I think you said such researches cost money."

"I'll find it, don't you fear. And there's other things I'll do, too. For instance, that guy Holden. I'll get him, I'll make him like me before I get done. There's a guy. But the first thing—I'm starting my life work. It's the kind of life work that doesn't show a profit, but never mind that. It's worth doing. Well—so it takes money. Well—then I'll get it. All right, I'm off. I didn't expect you to take me in your arms. But you'll be hearing from me—soon."

I didn't want him to go. I wanted him to stay, so I could quarrel with him until I was ready to make up. So when he picked up his hat, I jumped up. "Well—if you're looking for money, I think I can give you a name."

I went to the mantel where the envelope with the money in it was lying, having been entirely forgotten during the rather hasty exit taken by his mother. It had my name typed on it, and I handed it to him. "...What's this?"

167

"A name. I think she'll be good for anything you need."

He opened it, and when he saw what was inside he caught his breath. "Oh—the tip."

"Yes, but it's really yours. She's cheated you out of it."

I lay down on the sofa and he came and put the envelope on the table in front of me. "I didn't quite get you at first. No, it's yours. I can't take money off you, Carrie."

"Do you mean it about the Indians, or not?"

"Of course. But—"

"Then you take things any way you can get them." Then I added: "That's what *I* always do," and raised my foot in a very provocative way and began to wave it around in the air. So the next second I was in his arms, and there had never been any quarrel, or any Lula, or any mother, only him and me. So I spent the week-end in sin, and it was Sunday afternoon before I remembered I was supposed to spend it at Mrs. Jerome's, and we laughed and laughed because now I was a social celebrity, but had forgotten to show up.

■   ■   ■

I returned now to our sloop, which isn't anchored off the Bay Islands any more, but off Puerto Cortez, where our equipment is due tonight on a freighter, and tomorrow we start into the interior, for excavations and I don't know what-all. We spent two weeks in sin, as a matter of fact, at Atlantic City and a lot of places, for it took all sorts of red tape before Grant could get a license in New York. He had to prove the divorce was not granted against him on the ground of infidelity, or something. He kept his promise about Mr. Holden, and we all became good friends, and I don't think Mr. Holden felt hurt any more. We spent some time getting ready for the expedition, and it took a lot of my money, but I don't care. Tomorrow, Grant says, we start a perfectly hellish life, with mosquitoes, snakes, heat and everything else to bother us, and I guess it will be hard. But tonight there will be the Caribbean moon, and as it dances across the water, I shall think of the Modern Cinderella, and pretend that the light on the waves is really the silver slipper falling into her lap.